<u>Preface</u>

In 'Let's Pull Strings,' the narrative unfolds across the complex and layered world of business, personal relationships, and the struggles to find identity and meaning. This book is a reflection on ambition, mistakes, and the power of human connection. Through a thoughtful and introspective journey, it delves into themes of leadership, loyalty, and the challenges faced in modern corporate life.

I hope readers find not only entertainment in these pages, but also inspiration to reflect on their own paths and choices.

Welcome to the journey!

Things to Follow

Conundrum

"Mr. Shovik, the losses keep piling up every quarter, and none of your strategies seem to be making a difference. If this continues, the board may have to explore options that don't include you."

"What do you mean 'beyond me'? Don't forget, my father founded this company. I may not have a majority stake, but I'm still the largest shareholder."

"I apologize for my outburst. I got a little carried away. I want the board to know I'm still fully committed to restoring this company's reputation, and I'll do everything in my power to make it happen."

"Mr. Shovik, the board still has faith in you—for now. But if the losses continue, that confidence could evaporate quickly. As CEO, you have a huge responsibility. You need to step up, big time."

"Yes, I understand, Mr. Oberoi."

"With that, the Annual General Meeting is adjourned. Thank you all for attending. I'm Amal Oberoi, Chief Board Secretary, and I hope we see better days ahead."

"Where's Shovik?"
"He's still in the boardroom, sir."
"Still? It's been eight hours since the AGM ended! What on earth is he doing in there?"

"Shovik, what's going on? Why are you still sitting here?"

"Father, the board questioned my ability to lead this company. Can you believe that?"

"Really? And they should have. I've told the board before—they've been too easy on you."

"What are you saying, Father?"

"I'm saying three straight quarters of heavy losses, with no external excuses like the economy or supply chain issues, is absurd. If I were on that board, I would've fired you."

"You can't be serious!"

"Dead serious. This company has been in business for over 25 years and has been a leader in the hospitality industry. Suddenly, we're out of ideas and can't draw in business? That's unacceptable. We've got nearly 20,000 employees working for us—are you telling me not a single one of them can figure this out? It doesn't add up."

"Father, I have a small, tight-knit team working on strategies."

"That's part of the problem. Have you ever thought about tapping into ideas from the lower levels of the company?"

"Well, we do have the annual CEO meet-and-greet where I connect with new talent and a select few employees."

"That's not what I mean. I'm talking about setting up formal meetings with employees to discuss real issues and brainstorm ideas."

"That's not practical, Father."

"Okay, then have you ever tried working with HR to identify employees with creative, out-of-the-box thinking?"

"No, nothing like that."

"Shovik, being a CEO is like being the captain of a sports team. And in football or cricket, a captain's job isn't just to pick the top players—it's about building the right team. Here's the trick: if you think selecting the best based on stats or records alone will win the game, you're mistaken. Sometimes, you need players who are unpredictable. They may not be consistent, but when they show up, they can win you the game."

"Unpredictable players? You're joking, right?"

"No, I'm serious. There will be a match where your top players just don't perform. It might even be the final match. And on that day, it'll be the wildcard player who shines. In cricket, we call them exciting players. The ones who keep the audience on the edge of their seats."

"So, you're saying I need an 'unpredictable player' in my team?"

"Exactly. Your current team might be great, but even the best teams need a player like that. It could change everything."

"How can you be so sure? Did you have a player like that when you built this company?"

"Yes, son, I did have someone like that, and believe it or not, much of the company you see today was built because of him."

"This can't be true! How come I never knew about this person?"

"Oh, you know him, Shovik. It's just that the context is different."

"Now I'm really curious. I'd love to hear about him. Tell me his story."

"First, grab us both a coffee. And make sure the sugar's right, or I'm not saying a word."

"Here's your coffee, Father. Now, let's get to it."

"What happened, Uncle Param? Why are you crying?"

"Aarav, they took away my home..."

"Who? The bank? But you never used the house as collateral, right?"

"I lied, Aarav. I did use it as collateral. I needed money for my daughter's education abroad. She's happily married now, but I lost my home—the house my Laxmi built with her own hands."

"Does Arya know about this?"

"No, and she never will. I don't want her to worry. Besides, she never calls me. The only one I talk to is you, Aarav."

"Uncle, you can't lose your home. That house is all you have left of Laxmi."

"I know, son. But I don't know how to get it back. How can I save the only thing I have of her?"

"Don't worry, Uncle. I won't let you become homeless after everything you've done for me."

"I haven't done much for you, Aarav."

"Are you kidding? You gave me a place to stay and treated me like family when I had no one. That's more than most would do these days. How much money do you need to pay the debt?"

"Three crores, Aarav, in one year."

"I'll figure something out. I promise you'll get your home back. But where are you staying for now?"

"With my sister, Aarav. Don't worry about me."

"Aarav, where did you disappear to?"

"I went to see Uncle Param. The bank took his house, and he's heartbroken."

"That's rough. So, what's the plan?"

"Three crores, Shravan. That's the number he needs."

"Whoa, that's a huge amount."

"I know, but I can't let them take the house. It's like my home too."

"Aarav, listen. You and I are orphans. Uncle Param gave you a roof over your head, but let's be real—you weren't his son. You were more like a servant."

"That's not true, Shravan. He gave me schooling just like his own child."

"Did he? You never even went to school. You just took the exams at the end of the year because his friend was the principal."

"Still, he provided me with something. That wasn't free, Shravan. I worked hard, yes, but it wasn't just labor—it was a real chance."

"Man, you're always so practical, except when it comes to this. I don't get why you see Uncle Param's family as your own. You were just a servant to them."

"You'll never understand, Shravan. Let's just drop it."

"Okay, okay. You're my brother, and if you think it's right, I'm with you."

"Now let's go. We're late for work, and in case you forgot, we're waiters—not the owners. We can't be late."

"Where are we working today?"

"Some family functions. Again."

"Not another one! I hate catering gigs. Why can't I just stay at the restaurant?"

"Come on, man. It's been 15 days since you joined, and I had to convince you since no one was hiring you after your BBA."

"Yeah, because I got my BBA from an open university. Nobody takes that seriously."

"And your fancy English didn't help you land a job either, huh?"

"They never even interviewed me. Just rejected my resume right away."

"Exactly what I said when you choose that course. You wasted three years."

"Leave it. We've argued enough about this. Let's just get moving."

"Alright, everyone! As you know, we've landed the biggest catering gig of the year. It's the family function of billionaire Mr. Shaurya Sen. He's one of the top industrialists in the country, with businesses in oil, gas, semiconductors, and now telecom. Our company, Ahuja Sons, has a longstanding relationship with him, so consider this like our own family event. We cannot afford any slip-ups—our reputation in the hospitality industry is on the line. Are we clear?"

"Yes, sir!" the staff shouted in unison.

"Why does it always feel like we're preparing for war before every event?"

"Because, man, Ahuja Sons' reputation is at stake."

"This speech is so old, I could probably recite it in my sleep."

"By the way, have you noticed how empty the main restaurant's been? Is it the same with the others?"

"Yeah, their business is sinking. All those little fast-food joints on every corner are stealing customers left and right."

"Hey, how do I look?"

"Wow, Prince Aarav, you look like... a waiter. If that's what you wanted to hear, no pun intended."

"Come on, Sri, not even a second of, 'You look handsome'?"

"Oh, handsome, huh? Hate to break it to you, but your looks don't count when you're a waiter with a pocket full of holes."

"Sri, you're the rudest guy I've ever known."

"You mean honest, right, Aarav?"

"Yeah, whatever. Let's just go save our boss's reputation."

"Don't joke, man. It's not the time for laughs."

"Alright, alright. Let's get to work."

Serving drinks and snacks to the guests

"Well, well, look who it is—Mr. CEO of Sen Telecom himself, the dashing Lakshya Seth!"

"Pragya! Long time no see!"

"Yeah, that's because you've been busy becoming CEO the moment you left college!"

"It wasn't like that. I came back home, and you stayed in the U.S., so, you know... time zones didn't exactly line up."

"At least make up excuses that are easier to believe!"

"You know I'm bad at this."

"Never mind. I'm just really proud of you. One of my best friends is now a top CEO in the country. And Uncle Sen trusting you with the whole telecom division? That's amazing!"

"Yeah, Mr. Sen's a great guy. If he believes in you, he's got your back, no question. Making me CEO over his own son wasn't an easy decision."

"Speaking of which, where's Shivanya?"

"I think she hasn't arrived yet."

"Oh, wait—there she is. Look, Mr. CEO, she's walking in now. She's stunning, isn't she?"

"Yeah, Pragya, she's the best."

"Hmm, is that why you're in love with her?"

"What? Who said that? It's not like that!"

"Really? Because the rumors are swirling that you two are into each other, and Mr. Sen seems to like you too."

"I mean, we just get along really well. That's all."

"Uh-huh. Well, I'm rooting for you two. As Shivanya's childhood friend, I can tell you—you're a perfect match."

"Hi, Pragya!"

"Hi, Shivanya! You look amazing!"

"Thanks, Pragya. You too!"

"Hi, Lakshya."

"Hey, Shivanya. Looking beautiful as always."

"Tell me something I don't know."

"Hey, waiter!"

"Yes, sir?"

"Bring me a vodka sip."

"Right away, sir."

"Vivaan, bro, look! Shivanya's here. Already making her entrance. She's gorgeous, isn't she?"

"Yeah, man, she's stunning. But don't forget—Lakshya's got dibs on her. He's our bro, remember?"

"Bro, Shravan, who's Shivanya?"

"Dude, the girl right there in the black dress. Turn around."

"Wow, she's... beautiful."

"Aarav, what's up? You're frozen, man. Stop staring, she'll notice!"

"Sri, she's... she's breathtaking. Is this real?"

"Oh, hold on! Is Mr. Emotionless falling for someone?"

"No, no, it's not like that. It's just that she's... enchanting. Her eyes shine like stars."

"Well, well! We've got a poet now! But listen, Aarav, admire all you want, but don't fall for her. She's like the moon—beautiful to look at, but untouchable. Definitely not someone you can have."

"It's not like that, Sri..."

"Waiter, where's my drink?"

"Coming, sir. Here you go, Aarav. Serve that guy."

"Hey, you! That's my drink!"

"Sorry, sir, this one's for someone else. I'll get you another."

As I turned, I accidentally collided with Shivanya.

"You idiot! What were you thinking? You just spilled the drink all over my arm and my bangle!"

"Sorry, ma'am. I was just distracted for a moment and didn't see you coming."

"So, you're saying it's my fault now?"

"No, not at all, ma'am. I'll get some napkins and water for you right away."

"So you can spill more on me? Unbelievable."

"What happened, Shivanya?"

"This idiot spilled a drink on me, Lakshya."

"You, waiter—who let you serve drinks without any manners? You don't get it, do you?"

"Are you okay, Shivanya?"

"Yeah, Lakshya, I'm fine."

"I should fire you right now. This catering service is a joke if they hire people like you. You can't even handle a simple task. You're worthless!"

"Lakshya, calm down. I'm fine. My dad's looking for me anyway."

"Alright, but I don't want to see this guy again."

"I'll take care of it."

"Come with me. Look, I respect and love Ahuja Uncle, which is the only reason I'm not making a bigger deal of this. But fools like you can't be ruining his catering service. What's your name?"

"Aarav, ma'am."

"Wow, fancy name. Do you even know who I am?"

"No, ma'am."

"I'm Shivanya Sen, daughter of the biggest industrialist in India. What happened here wasn't a mistake. You were lost in your own world, not paying attention."

"Listen, I don't usually waste my energy yelling at people like you. What's your salary?"

"10,000 rupees, ma'am."

"Do you even know how much this bangle you spilled your drink on costs? It would take you 5,000 years to earn enough to buy it with your salary. That's how valuable it is."

"I'm sorry, ma'am."

"Is 'sorry' the only English word you know? Your sorry means nothing, so don't bother saying it."

"And by the way, I saw you staring at me earlier."

"No, ma'am, I wasn't staring. I was looking somewhere else."

"Shut up. Don't lie. Never look at a woman like that again. Understood?"

"Yes, ma'am."

"And one more thing—leave right now and don't come back tomorrow. I'm going to call Ahuja Uncle and make sure you're fired. Got it?"

"Yes, ma'am."

Shivanya and Maya's Conversation

Shivanya walked away from the commotion when Maya caught up with her.

"Shivanya, what happened back there?"

"Nothing, Maya."

"So... you and Lakshya, huh?"

"No, Maya, it's not like that."

"Oh, so you don't like him?"

"I didn't say that. Lakshya is a great guy—he's done his MBA in the US, came back to live with his parents, and he's incredibly work-oriented. The way he's handled our new telecom business has been outstanding. His ideas and the way he implements them are just perfect."

"Wow, sounds like someone's a little smitten."

"Not exactly, but yes, he's different. I always wanted someone focused, grounded, and someone who'd stay in India to help my father with the business. Lakshya fits that perfectly."

"He's definitely not like those spoiled rich boys with terrible habits. I like him for you, Shivanya."

"Yeah... maybe."

Mr. Sen and Mr. Rao's Conversation

"Shivanya, come here," Mr. Sen called out.

"Yes, father, right away."

Mr. Rao, one of the guests, turned to Mr. Sen with a smile.

"Mr. Sen, you've really taken the telecom industry by storm with Emilink, and appointing Lakshya as CEO was a masterstroke. Not just the stakeholders but the public also loves him. Should we be expecting some good news between Shivanya and Lakshya soon?"

"Mr. Rao, Shivanya is still young and has just returned after completing her MBA. Let her spend some time with her father first. Lakshya is a fine match for her, but when the time is right, we'll make the announcement."

Mr. Sen's Speech

Mr. Sen approached the stage and grabbed the mic.

"Ladies and gentlemen, I, Shaurya Sen, welcome you all to the success party of Emilink, our telecom venture. Emilink now holds the largest customer base in the country, surpassing the previous market leader in just two years. Full credit goes to our CEO and the entire Emilink team. I'd like to invite Lakshya Seth to address the gathering."

Applause erupted as Lakshya walked to the stage.

"Thank you, sir. Your words mean a lot to me."
The crowd cheered loudly, making it hard for Lakshya to start his speech. He smiled and folded his hands in a respectful "namaste" before continuing.

"I'm overwhelmed by this warm reception. When I returned to India, many people told me I'd regret it. They said, 'Why come back when everyone is settling abroad?' But I always saw India as a land of immense potential.

"When I joined Emilink as AVP of Strategy and Implementation, I knew the Indian telecom market was fiercely competitive, especially with Indian customers—they're a tough crowd. Our strategy was simple: make SIM cards easily accessible. We set up small kiosks in every city so people didn't have to go far to get a SIM card—just like grabbing street food. You could get a SIM card on almost every corner. This approach worked wonders. We also focused on Tier 2 and Tier 3 cities, setting up pocket centers with hotspots in each region.

"The results have been incredible. In just two years, Emilink is now the leader in the telecom sector. I want to use this opportunity to thank everyone at Emilink for their hard work in making this happen so quickly.

"India is vast, and there's still a lot of room to grow, especially when it comes to logistics and supply chains. I promise, the next time we gather, Emilink will be a giant in this industry, with numbers beyond imagination in terms of customers and business."

Lakshya paused and looked at the audience.
"And finally, a huge thank you to Mr. Sen for giving me the chance to lead Emilink as its CEO. My heartfelt thanks to everyone here tonight. Thank you so much!"

The crowd applauded as Lakshya stepped down from the stage.

<u>Pull is Missing</u>

Aarav sat brooding after the humiliating incident with Shivanya. His friend, Sri, noticed.

"Why are you sitting here like this?" Sri asked.

"You saw what happened last night, and you're still asking?" Aarav replied.

"Forget it, Aarav. Typical rich-people behavior. Looks like today's the last day of your job, huh?"

"Yeah, it seems like it. Let's just go home—the party's over anyway."

The Next Morning

Sri was shouting in the morning.

"Aarav, wake up! We're getting late for work!"

"You're getting late, Sri. I got fired last night, remember? Thanks to the beautiful Shivanya."

"Well, I got a message from the boss. He said you need to report to the restaurant, and I have to handle the catering function."

"Why? Is he planning to rub more salt into my wound? And unlike Shivanya, he's definitely not as pleasing to look at."

"It sounds like Shivanya is living rent-free in your head."

"She's so beautiful, Sri, and those eyes... they were filled with so much truth. It was like looking at a reflection of my soul."

"Hello, Mr. Poet! Did you forget she insulted you? She said you were 5,000 years behind her. And yet here you are, daydreaming about her."

"Sri, anyone who shows you your place in this world is actually helping you."

"What? How?"

"Well, now I know I have 5,000 years to cover. She's quantified my brokenness."

"Get serious, Aarav. Remember your promise to Param Uncle."

"Yes, Sri. I will never forget my promises."

"And why didn't you stand up for yourself in front of her?"

"I wanted to, Sri. But the moment I heard her voice, I was completely tongue-tied."

"And you speak some of the finest English I know! Yet you let her tell you that you didn't know the language. You were better off before you joined me in the restaurant business."

"Don't blame yourself, Sri. You did a great job bringing me here. That's why I like you."

"Well, get ready to face more insults, courtesy of Shivanya."

"I guess I will. Let's go. Drop me off at the restaurant."

At the Restaurant

Aarav entered the restaurant, hesitant.

"May I come in, sir?"

"You're late, Aarav," the manager said.

"Sorry, sir. I thought I was fired last night."

"You almost were. My father told me to fire you, but I told him that I invest too much in training my staff to let them go over one mistake—especially one that wasn't even your fault. Shivanya is... let's just say, I know how she can be."

"Thank you, sir," Aarav replied, relieved.

"Now join us for this briefing."

Neil Ahuja's Open Forum

Neil Ahuja, the CEO of the restaurant chain, addressed the room.

"As you all know, my father gave me an ultimatum. We need to turn a profit. It's been two years without any growth. That's why I've organized this open forum. I don't like closed-door meetings—everything should be transparent and communicated to the team."

He paused, surveying the room.

"Despite being in prime locations and offering the best food, we're losing to smaller, more agile competitors. 'Quick Snacks' started as a street outlet, and now they own an entire space! Even my father's so-called friend Mr. Sen has invested in them. I keep telling my father, in business, you have no friends—only competition. But he still believes in relationships."

Aarav, sitting at the back, whispered to a colleague, "How long has this lecture been going on?"

"Since early morning," the colleague replied.

"And what are we supposed to do? We're waiters—how can we help with business strategy?"

"Apparently, Neil likes to sit with people and find his 'Eureka' moments," the colleague said.

"You're kidding, right?" Aarav asked, skeptical.

"No, seriously."

Neil noticed the conversation and snapped, "You two at the back, are we running a circus here? Care to share what's so interesting?"

"Sorry, sir," Aarav mumbled.

"Sorry for what? Do I have to shout to make you understand the gravity of the situation? We're discussing how to save this business, and you two are busy gossiping!"

He turned to Aarav.

"And Aarav, don't think I won't fire you. If you can't contribute, at least have the decency to listen."

"Sorry, sir!" Aarav said.

Neil sighed. "No, it's my fault for expecting you to understand. What could you possibly know about business?"

That was it. Aarav had had enough.

"Actually, sir," Aarav interrupted, "I know more than you think."

"What did you just say?" Neil asked, surprised.

"I said, I've had enough of the insults. You want to know why your business is failing? Let me tell you. I'm a waiter, yes, but I also recently completed my BBA."

Neil raised an eyebrow. "A BBA, huh? Go on, then. Tell me what I'm missing."

Aarav's Bold Pitch and Neil's Decision

Aarav stood his ground, eyes blazing.

"The pull is missing," he declared.

Neil frowned. "What pull?"

"Your restaurants don't have the pull that attracts customers."

"And what exactly is this 'pull,' Mr. Aarav, BBA? If you care to explain."

Joe, visibly irritated, jumped in. "How dare you speak to our boss like this?"

Neil raised his hand to calm him down. "Relax, Joe. Let's hear what he has to say. Go on, Aarav. Explain your 'pull' to everyone."

Aarav took a deep breath.

"Neil, what brand of phone do you own?"

"An Omega 5," Neil replied.

"And why Omega, and not some other brand?"

"Because Omega is the best in its segment. It protects my privacy, and its unique system can't be easily hacked. It stands apart from the other brands, which all run on the same platform. Everyone wants an Omega."

Aarav nodded. "Exactly. That's the pull. Omega stands out because it offers something desirable, something others can't. The stronger the pull, the stronger the attraction—and that's how you bring in staggering numbers of customers."

He paused for effect, then continued.

"Now, tell me, what pull do your restaurants have? Let's start with the name—'Ahuja Luxury Family Restaurant.' You think that's going to draw the youth of today? No. The only people who come to your restaurant are middle-aged or older. Meanwhile, there's a club nearby that's packed with young people all day long."

Aarav's words stung, but Neil listened intently.

"If you don't create a pull, Neil, these losses will turn into debts, and soon, this restaurant will shut down. And when this one goes, so will the others—it's your main branch. You need to act fast."

Aarav exhaled sharply. "I've given you all the advice I can. Now, if you'll excuse me, I've been hearing about getting fired since yesterday. I'll save you the trouble—I quit."

He turned toward the door, but Neil's voice stopped him.

"Wait, Aarav! How dare you leave like this, especially when you know how to fix the problem? Isn't it your responsibility to help?"

"Neil," Aarav said softly, "I respect you. You've helped me when I was struggling, but I feel like I'm out of options."

"No, Aarav, you do have a choice," Neil said, standing up. "What if I told you that I want you to join me? If this works out, I'll make you COO. We'll be partners—not just employee and boss."

Aarav blinked, shocked. "You're not serious, Neil."

"I am," Neil said. "From the moment you joined, I knew you had something special. Now I see what it is."

They shook hands and hugged, tears in their eyes.

"You don't worry, Neil. I'll make this business bigger and better than your father ever dreamed," Aarav said confidently.

"I have complete faith in you," Neil replied. "Tomorrow, we'll start working on two things: creating that pull and building a product that supports it."

Back on the Terrace

Later that night, Sri came home, puzzled by what he'd heard at the restaurant.

"Aarav, where are you?"

"Up on the terrace," Aarav called back.

"Is it true, what I heard today? That you're working with Neil to save the business?" Sri asked, incredulous.

"Yes, it's true," Aarav said calmly.

"Are you out of your mind? You have no experience in turning around a business like this, and you think you can take on giants in the market?"

"Sri, I understand your worry," Aarav said. "But remember what you told me about the promise I made to Param Uncle. This is the only way to keep that promise."

"But what if things don't go as planned, Aarav? Have you thought about what those businessmen might do to you? I don't want to lose you over some promise. You're like the only family I have left."

Aarav placed a hand on Sri's shoulder. "I know, Sri. And I've thought about the risks. But I can't back down now. This is bigger than just me."
Sri sighed, conflicted but trusting his brother's determination. "Alright, Aarav. Just promise me you'll be careful."

Setting the Stage for the "Pull"

The next morning, Aarav was ready to set his plan in motion.

Neil, curious and a bit cautious, asked, "So Aarav, where do we start?"
"First, we temporarily shut down our main branch," Aarav replied confidently.
"Why would we do that?" Neil asked, puzzled.
"I'll explain. Joe," Aarav continued, turning to the manager, "get big hoardings set up all over NCR's hotspots. The banners should say, 'Ahuja Luxury Restaurant, Main Branch, Saket—Temporarily Shut. We'll be back soon with a bang. Stay tuned.'"

Joe nodded, taking notes. "Got it, Aarav. And I'll make sure the design is catchy."
"Exactly. It needs to grab attention, but not too much. We want our competitors to think something's up, that we're down but trying to get back up. It'll buy us time to renovate without them catching wind of our real plans."

Neil's eyes lit up as he began to understand.
"So, you're letting them believe we're struggling? So, they relax and let their guard down, thinking they've already won."
"Exactly, boss," Aarav grinned. "Once they're basking in their supposed victory, we'll hit them with our surprise."

"Alright, I like it," Neil said, impressed. "But we need to be prepared with a solid plan. Once these banners go up, my father and everyone else will be on my case."

"Don't worry, boss," Aarav assured him. "The plan is ready. But until we launch, I suggest you keep your answers vague—tell them we're 'working on something.' Let them wonder."

Neil chuckled. "I guess you're setting me up for more insults, Aarav."
"Maybe a little," Aarav smiled. "But remember, 'the greater the loss, the sweeter the profit.'"
Neil raised an eyebrow. "You're full of surprises today."

The Two-Product Strategy

"So, what's the plan for revamping the restaurant?" Neil asked, leaning forward.
"Well, our restaurant has two sides—north and east," Aarav began.
"Yes, it does," Neil nodded.
"We're going to create two restaurants under one banner," Aarav said.

Neil blinked. "Two restaurants? Are you serious? The loss of one wasn't enough?"
"It's not what you think," Aarav said. "We'll offer two distinct products in the same space, targeting different customers. And the best part is, we have the room to pull it off."

Neil was intrigued. "Okay, explain the philosophy behind this."

"The idea is to offer two experiences: one premium, and the other more casual and youthful," Aarav explained. "Think of it like clothing brands. You wear premium brands, right?"
"Of course," Neil nodded.
"But do you always buy the most exclusive, celebrity-endorsed items?" Aarav asked.
"Well, not always. Sometimes I go for something a bit cheaper, depending on the category."
"Exactly. Premium brands do this all the time. They offer high-end, exclusive products to maintain their prestige, but they also offer a second, more affordable line for the middle class."

Aarav leaned in, his energy building. "No business can thrive without tapping into the middle and upper-middle-class segments. Premium brands use celebrities as marketing tools, but their real profits come from products that appeal to the broader market. These slightly more affordable lines are still priced higher than local competitors, but they ride on the brand's 'pull.' The customers believe they're getting something superior, validated by the price tag."

Neil listened intently as Aarav continued.
"For example, a t-shirt that could be made locally for ₹1,000 is sold by these brands for ₹10,000 or ₹20,000, simply because of the brand name. The design may be only slightly different, but the margins? They're through the roof."

Neil leaned back, impressed. "So, you want to take that same strategy and apply it to our restaurant?"
"Exactly," Aarav nodded. "We'll have one premium dining experience and one casual, trendy space. We'll attract two different crowds without losing the brand's pull."

Neil grinned, clearly impressed. "Alright, Aarav. Let's do it."

The Psychology of the Pull

"So, it's all about playing with price and human psychology, right? That's how brands become multimillion-dollar companies?" Neil asked, still digesting Aarav's strategy.

"Exactly," Aarav confirmed.
Neil was amazed. "I'm impressed by your observation skills. How did you figure all this out?"
"It's pretty obvious once you start looking at things deeply," Aarav said with a smile.

"Alright, so we have two products: a premium and a profit-focused one. The east side will be for profit, and the north side will be premium. The east is closer to the road, so it'll be more eye-catching, while the north, being more private, is perfect for a premium setting."

Neil nodded, his confidence growing. "Okay, the plan sounds good. What about the theme for both sides?"

"That's the most important part," Aarav said. "Oh, and I've already called an interior designer to discuss it."

Neil raised an eyebrow. "I know a lot of designers. I could get the best for us."

"We don't need someone with too much experience," Aarav said.

"Why not?" Neil asked, surprised.

"Because experienced designers are often influenced by their past work. Their designs may be great, but they lack the freshness we need. A fresher designer brings new ideas, which will help us stand out."

Neil nodded thoughtfully. "Makes sense. So, who is it?"

"Her name is Shabby Arora. She comes from a wealthy family, so she's a bit pricey."

"I'll handle the cost," Neil said. "But why Shabby?"

"She's motivated to prove herself to her father and build something of her own, despite coming from money. That drive and hunger are exactly what we need," Aarav explained.

Neil was intrigued. "How do you know her?"

"I met her at a creative forum where she was a speaker. I used the Ahuja family name to convince her to take the job. She knows if this works out, it'll make her a name in the industry."

Just then, Shabby arrived. "Hi Aarav, am I late?" she asked with a playful tone.

"Not really. But even if you were, I'd never expect you to be on time," Aarav joked.

Shabby grinned. "Good. And don't expect it in the future either!" She turned to Neil. "You must be the boss. Or something like that."

Neil smiled. "More like I just manage things."

"I see," Shabby smirked. "And this is Joe, the manager, right?"

"Yes, I am. Nice to meet you," Joe said.

"Just call me Shabby, none of that 'madam' stuff."

"Alright, Shabby," Joe replied, trying to keep up with her energy.

Shabby turned back to Neil. "And you, Neil, I'll just call you by your name. I don't do 'boss' titles."

"Call me anything you like," Neil chuckled.

"Where's my coffee, Aarav? You know I can't function without it," Shabby asked.

"Coming right up," Aarav said, heading off to get it.

Shabby looked around the restaurant. "So, Neil, you were involved in the last renovation?"

"Yes," Neil said, clearly proud.

"Well, no offense, but this place sucks," Shabby said bluntly.

Neil laughed. "That's why you're here, Shabby."

"Seems like not just the place needs renovating—you might need it too, Neil Ahuja," she teased.

Neil was taken aback. "Me? I need renovating?"

Shabby grinned. "Yeah, your memory for one. You were terrible as a kid, and it's still the same!"

Neil was confused. "Wait, what? How do you know me from childhood?"

"Remember a girl named Shreya Arora from your school?" Shabby asked.

Neil's eyes widened. "Yes, the topper. The one I… always admired."

"Yes, the same one you stalked with those gloomy eyes but never had the guts to approach," Shabby said with a playful smirk.

"How do you know all this?" Neil asked, stunned.

"Because, idiot, I am Shreya Arora. Shabby is just my business name."

Neil was in shock. "Shreya… this can't be real."

"Oh, it's real, Neil," Shabby said, enjoying his surprise.

Aarav returned with the coffee. "Here's your coffee, Shabby."

"Thanks, Aarav," she said, taking a sip.

Neil, still trying to process everything, turned to Aarav. "Did you know she's my schoolmate?"

Aarav grinned. "Yeah, the one you couldn't stop talking about when you were drunk."

Shabby laughed. "Oh, really? I'll deal with you later, Neil."

"Let's focus on the work first," Shabby said, changing the tone. "I've brought some sample designs for the north side. Since you want a premium feel, I've gone with a nature-inspired theme. We'll use light-colored walls, elegant props like paintings, and premium furniture made from light wood. The lighting will be soft and soothing, perfect for a high-end dining experience."

Neil looked at the designs. "This looks fantastic, Shabby."
Aarav nodded in agreement. "I love it. But let's add one more thing—a piano."
"A piano?" Neil asked, surprised.
"Yes, we'll have a live pianist in the evenings to add to the atmosphere. It'll elevate the experience."
"Good idea," Neil agreed.

"We'll also keep the hours from noon to midnight to cater to different crowds," Aarav added.
"Sounds perfect," Neil said, clearly impressed.

The Final Countdown: Design and Branding

"Shabby, the design looks fantastic and is approved from our side. How many days will you need to implement this?" Aarav asked, eager to get the ball rolling.

"At least 15 days," Shabby replied confidently.
"Ten days max," Aarav countered, pushing for a tighter schedule.
"Sorry, Aarav, but 15 days was already tight. Ten days is impossible!" she exclaimed.
"Shreya, please," Neil insisted, trying to help.
"What do you want, Neil? Just because you're asking doesn't mean I'll budge. I'm not your girlfriend, so don't expect any unnecessary favors," Shabby retorted.

"I need something in return," she continued.
"What are you thinking?" Neil asked.

"I want you to sign a contract making me the official designer for all your restaurants and upcoming outlets. I want this opportunity to prove myself," Shabby declared.

"But Shabby, it's not easy! I need my father's approval since he's the primary stakeholder," Neil explained.

"That's your headache, not mine. I see an opportunity and I want to make it big, just like you two," she replied, determined.

Neil thought it over. "Okay, it's a deal, but only if this project pays off as expected. If it fails because of your mistake, I don't want to suffer unnecessarily."

"No promises on that front, but if this works out, you'll have me on board for the entire Ahuja Sons group—offices, hotels, and restaurants. It's a promise," Shabby assured him.

"Seems fair to me. It's done then," she concluded.

"Alright, so it's settled: 10 days to launch. Now, can you show us the theme for the eastern side?" Aarav asked, shifting focus.

"Here's the concept!" Shabby replied, showing off the vibrant design. "This theme features casual seating areas, including a dedicated gaming section and a cozy movie night corner. We'll have a huge screen for games and movies, with seating options like bean bags and couches. The ceiling will be designed to resemble a scenic night sky, creating an open-theater vibe for friends to gather."

"Looks great, Shabby!" Neil commented.

"Yes, it's a complete space for everyone. The eastern side will cater to youth, couples looking for privacy, and anyone wanting a fun gathering spot," Aarav added.

"Exactly, Aarav! Plus, the two sides will differ dramatically in outlook, food, and pricing," Shabby explained.

"The northern side will have a premium menu with higher prices, while the eastern side will feature slightly elevated prices that are still justified. The customers will champion this pricing model, just wait and see," Aarav said confidently.

"Great job, Shabby. Thanks for putting this all together so quickly—it really shows your passion for the work," Neil said, finalizing the design with her input.

"Joe, it's on you to ensure the food is distinct for both sides. Just remember, the northern side should focus on cuisines like Italian and French," Aarav instructed.

"I remember a chef... what's his name? Chef Koel! He's renowned for his fusion dishes," Joe replied, excited.

"We'll have a special section in the menu featuring his creations for the northern side. Don't look confused, Joe. You have to get him on board. Offer him a price and share our vision—I'm sure he'll want to be a part of it," Aarav urged. "As for the eastern side, I know you're the best at putting together a fast-food menu, so you can handle that."

"Got it, Aarav! I'll make it happen," Joe confirmed.

"Remember, Joe, no food means no restaurant! This is not the time for trying; you must do it!" Aarav insisted.

"Understood!" Joe replied, energized.

"We've covered nearly all the bases for the renovation, but I still feel something is missing," Aarav said thoughtfully.

"Names!" Shabby shouted, catching on quickly. "What are we calling these two units? Names are crucial when it comes to pulling customers in."

"Yes! The names are essential!" Aarav agreed. "I already have the perfect name for the northern side—it's going to be called 'Ambrosia.'"

"Wow, that's unique, Aarav! It perfectly fits the theme," Shabby exclaimed.

"What does Ambrosia mean?" Neil asked.

"It's a Greek word for the food of the gods," Aarav explained.

"That's brilliant, Aarav! You nailed it!" Neil praised. "Now, what about the eastern side?"

"Kissaten," Joe suggested.

"Kissaten? What a great name! It has that alluring quality we're looking for," Aarav said, impressed.

"Perfect. So we have 'Ambrosia' for the northern side and 'Kissaten' for the eastern side. Guys, we have only ten days to make this happen. Let's show the world what we're capable of!" Aarav rallied the team.

"Absolutely!" Neil agreed, filled with excitement.

"Indeed! Let's do this!" Shabby added enthusiasm radiating from her.

With that, the team was ready to take on the challenge and transform their vision into reality.

The Challenge Ahead: Preparing for Success

"You got here a little late, Sri," Aarav remarked as he settled in.

"Yes, I know. This catering job was a nightmare. It felt like everyone was partying like it was their last day on Earth!" Sri replied, shaking his head.

"Forget about it," Aarav said, brushing it off. "On my way back, I found out our restaurant is getting shut down temporarily."

"Is that right? Is this your doing, Aarav?" Sri asked, surprised.

"Yes, it is. We have ten days to make this place something special."

"Oh, I see. Mr. COO is suddenly in entrepreneur mode," Sri teased.

"Exactly. But that means no holiday for us. We have to put in extra shifts to finish everything in ten days."

"What do you expect me to do, Mr. COO?" Sri asked, intrigued.

"You're our grooming instructor. I need you to prepare our staff to step up their service standards, especially for the premium side," Aarav explained.

"I heard the restaurant is getting divided into two halves," Sri noted.

"Yes, you'll see it all tomorrow when you get to the restaurant."

"I need the best-groomed professionals on our service staff," Aarav emphasized. "The premium side will operate like a five-star restaurant, and you know how high the service standards are in that environment. Our customers will expect nothing less, and we can't have issues like unattended tables or long waits for drinks. The service has to be timely and exceptional."

"You are the best grooming expert in the market, aren't you?"

"Yes, Sri, I know. You've worked in a five-star establishment too, so you understand the standards we need to meet."

"But Aarav," Sri said thoughtfully, "don't you think these restaurants might be out of touch with the kind of customers we usually attract? People here are always looking for heavy discounts and cheap deals. Can an ultra-luxury restaurant really work?"

"There's a fascinating aspect of human psychology at play, Sri," Aarav replied confidently. "People adapt to their surroundings. Sure, our local customers might be hesitant at first, but you'll see how this restaurant will attract corporate clients and the new generation. Once they start coming, the word will spread, not just locally but across the entire NCR region."

"Customers are always willing to elevate their standards for a premium experience. If they don't, it's the seller's fault for not providing the right product or service. Remember when everyone thought Omega phones would flop in India because they were too expensive? Now look—everyone wants one, and they're everywhere."

"So, whose fault is it if we fail to read customer behavior and their needs? Let me tell you, brands don't just create products based on customer requirements; they make sure to shape customer desires around what they produce. It's all about reverse psychology."

"I understand your point, Aarav," Sri conceded. "Now, I think it's time for both of us to get some rest. We've got an early start tomorrow."

"Absolutely, Sri. We need to be ready for what lies ahead," Aarav replied, a sense of determination settling in as they prepared for the ambitious project ahead.

T-10 Days to Launch: Team Progress and New Developments

"What's the status, guys?" Aarav inquired, scanning the room.

"Work in progress," Neil replied. "Shabby and I are sourcing renovation materials, while Joe is busy finalizing the menu."

"And Sri, as you all know, will start training our staff to improve their service proficiency."

"Great! That's one more member added to the team," Neil said, nodding in approval.

"While I was on my way to the restaurant, it struck me that we also need a social media manager to enhance our reach and market presence," Aarav continued.

"Hey Sri, remember that guy we met when we went to get your laptop fixed? The one working on gaming websites?"

"Yes, I remember. His father was pushing him to learn hardware repair instead of pursuing his passion," Sri recalled.

"That's the guy we need for social media management!" Aarav affirmed.

"How are you so sure he'll fit the role?" Neil questioned.

"Identifying the right talent is crucial for a successful entrepreneur. A strong team builds a strong business," Aarav explained.

"And it's equally important to give that talent the right space to grow and flourish," Neil added.

"Alright, I'll go get him and start building our social media presence," Aarav said, determined.

Aarav Meets Rishi's Father

Aarav approached the shop. "Excuse me, is anyone around?"

"Yes, how can I help you?" Shastri Ji asked.

"I'd like to speak to your son."

"Why? What's this about?"

"I have a job offer for him."

"A job for my son? How much does it pay?"

"80,000 per month."

"80,000? For my son?!" Shastri Ji exclaimed, surprised.

"Not exactly for your son, but for his talent," Aarav clarified.

"That's amazing! Rishi, come here!" Shastri Ji called.

"What's going on, Dad?" Rishi asked, intrigued.

"This gentleman has a job offer for you, paying 80,000 monthly!"

"How do you know me?" Rishi questioned, suspicious.

"I've seen your gaming site. The design is impressive. Once it's live, you could easily fetch more than what I'm offering from a sponsor," Aarav replied.

"What do you think? Just because I'm young, I don't know my worth?" Rishi snapped.

"Why are you saying this, son?" Shastri Ji asked, confused.

"Because they want to use my talent for their profits while offering me next to nothing. Just because I'm not earning right now doesn't mean this is a great opportunity."

"If that's true, why haven't you launched your site?" Aarav pressed.

"It will be live soon, I promise!" Rishi insisted.

"I'm impressed that you know your worth, but the site won't go live because its content is pirated. It's risky—there could be legal consequences if you proceed, especially from the gaming companies," Aarav explained. "Isn't that right, Rishi?"

"Is that true, Rishi?" Shastri Ji asked.

"No, Dad! He's lying!" Rishi protested.

"Rishi, you should be proud of valuing your upbringing over easy money," Aarav advised. "When we're young, we often think we can change the world overnight, but it takes time and effort. Maybe this opportunity is your first step toward that goal. Work as much as you can; it will benefit you in the long run."

"Are you ready to chase your dreams?" Aarav asked.

Rishi looked at his father, contemplating. "Okay, I'm ready."

"That's my boy! Don't worry, Shastri Ji, your son will achieve something great!" Aarav encouraged me.

Rishi Joins the Team

"So, what exactly will I be doing?" Rishi asked.

"I'm Aarav, and your KPIs will involve managing our social media platforms for the restaurant. I'll send you the designs and details you'll need. Create a buzz for our upcoming launch using tools like reels and other engaging content. Also, develop an app for reservations for our premium section."

"The app needs to be live before the launch—T-9 days. You'll have a dedicated office at the restaurant for corporate tasks," Aarav explained. "Make sure the app reflects the restaurant's premium vibe, with a similar color scheme. Come to me whenever you need more details. On T-9, you'll present your work on the app and social media front."

"Sounds good. I'll do my best!" Rishi replied.

"You could sound a bit more excited!" Aarav teased.

"I'll be excited when I see that paycheck," Rishi jokes.

"You're so mean! But anyways, good luck!" Aarav said, sharing a laugh with Rishi.

T-1 Day to Launch

Fast forward eight days, and they were now just T-1 days from the launch. The team was buzzing with energy and excitement, ready to showcase their hard work and creativity to the world.

Litmus Test

"You don't ever succeed in a business until you solve the riddle of execution."

After a grueling eight days of hard work, Aarav gathered the team for one final push. "Today marks our last day of preparation before we face the most critical challenge: the Execution Test," he stated solemnly. "Many refer to it as 'The Litmus Test.' All our efforts could go to waste if we don't nail this part. Starting tomorrow, it's all about addressing errors and making corrections."

He turned to Rishi. "What's the schedule for today?"
"We have a packed agenda to ensure we're ready," Rishi replied. "First, we'll tour the entire restaurant—both sides—with Shabby leading the way. Then, Neil will explain how both sections function and address any questions. After that, we'll have an app demo for both sides, followed by a team meeting to finalize the launch event details, which you will lead."

"Great! I assume everyone is clear on today's agenda?" Aarav asked, looking around. The team nodded in agreement, fueled by confidence.

The Tour Begins

"Alright, let's start with Shabby. Over to you," Aarav directed.
"Thanks, Aarav! Team, today you will witness the new restaurants for the first time. Are you excited? Never mind if you're not—by the end of this tour, you will be!" Shabby led them from the official space to the North side of the restaurant.

"Welcome to 'Ambrosia'—the place where every moment is an experience." The team gasped in awe at the sight before them. Ambrosia was a masterpiece, radiating luxury through its intricate design.

"The theme here beautifully fuses nature and light, with elegant white walls," Shabby explained. "We've incorporated an old-style giant wooden door that makes you feel like you're entering another world. Inside, you'll find a gallery filled with exotic art—my personal favorite is the Napoleon painting. Beyond that, there's a spacious hall with a dome-shaped ceiling that gives off a European vibe, complete with a magnificent chandelier at its center."

"At one end, you have the reception positioned amid the seating, ensuring an inviting atmosphere. The seating is arranged in small pockets for privacy, surrounded by plants to create boundaries. On either side of the reception, we have the kitchen and bar for efficient service, with wooden furniture complemented by luxurious leather seating for groups of four, as well as cozy chairs for smaller gatherings."

"Centered on the wall opposite the reception is a piano, and advanced music systems are installed throughout to enhance the ambiance. Every wall is adorned with paintings and antiques, including gramophones and old radios, as well as my favorite—pirate-style wooden ships. The seating area is strategically placed to ensure unobstructed service," Shabby continued, pride evident in his voice.

"I must say, Shabby, you truly have an eye for design. When you create something, it becomes a perfect piece of art," Aarav praised.
"Neil, what's your take?"
"I'm blown away by how you've transformed this space, Shabby. This dome structure was always here, but your reimagining of it is simply magical. I can't wait to see my father's reaction. The entrance design, with its lower-height stairs and elegant lamp posts, creates a regal first impression."
"This design was intentionally crafted to convey that this is no ordinary restaurant; it's special and will become the highlight of our establishment," Shabby explained.

"Restaurant? After seeing this, it's hard to believe it's just a restaurant. It feels like stepping into a palace," Joe remarked.

"That's precisely the idea—to redefine the concept of a restaurant in the modern world," Aarav agreed.

"Is everything ready for Ambrosia, Shabby?"

"Yes, Aarav, everything looks perfect. Just one thing: have we finalized the piano artist? He's a crucial element for the evening ambiance."

"Actually, I forgot, but he'll be here tomorrow," Shabby admitted.

"Make sure you arrange that, Aarav."

"Yes, Neil, I'll take care of it."

Moving On to the Eastern Side

"Now, let's head over to the Eastern side," Shabby continued. "I present to you 'The Kessanet'—a space where friends come together to celebrate their bonds, featuring a modern style with a premium touch."

"The entrance has a black door with a classic bell overhead, reminiscent of London style. The corridor is adorned with modern art, featuring paintings of legendary artists like Jim Morrison and Elvis."

"Upon entering the main hall, you'll notice a giant bar setup where only mocktails will be served—no alcohol. The bar serves as a decorative prop rather than a traditional bar," Shabby clarified. "This place is all about fun and excitement, in stark contrast to the tranquil Ambrosia. Scattered seating arrangements are designed for social interaction, complete with leather upholstery."

"The advanced sound system is akin to a theater setup, providing great bass to create a lively atmosphere. And for those who love dining under the stars, we have rooftop seating. There's even a dedicated area for movies and gaming featuring a large screen, bean bags, and couches. The ceiling mimics the constellations, making it a perfect hangout spot for friends."

As the tour wrapped up, the team felt the anticipation building. They were ready to tackle the Execution Test, knowing that their hard work and creativity had set the stage for a truly unique dining experience. With just one day left until the launch, excitement buzzed through the air as they prepared to unveil their vision to the world.

"Kessanet seems like the perfect spot to chill with friends," Aarav remarked. "Absolutely, that rooftop mini-private theater is a game changer!" Neil chimed in.

"Cool, Shabby!" Rishi added, acknowledging their excitement. "Everything looks ready to roll. Great job, Shabby!" Aarav said with a grin. "You know I excel at what I do," Shabby replied confidently.

"Awesome! We're all set on our end. Next up, Neil will walk us through how the restaurants will operate. Neil, take it away!" Aarav gestured for him to start.

"Thanks, Aarav. Team, let's gather in the meeting room so I can lay out how both restaurants will function.

First, we have 'Ambrosia.' Valet parking is standard at the entrance, and there will be a doorman to welcome guests. As visitors walk through the gallery, a dedicated waiter will assist them with their orders, ensuring the food comes straight from the kitchen, steaming hot. Both Ambrosia and Kessanet will offer a welcome drink—Kessanet's will be non-alcoholic. Guests will be asked for their drink preferences and served first before they place their orders. During the day, we'll play light music, with piano performances starting at 8 PM in the evening. If Aarav can snag a talented piano artist in time, we'll have quality jazz music to set the mood.

Rishi will cover the app side later today. Also, every table will have a tablet-sized screen displaying the menu—no physical menus! Once a guest selects their order, the chef will get a notification on a central wall screen, letting the serving staff know when to pick up the dishes. We'll be using a cart system for serving, so no more balancing trays on hands. The theme is clear: blending tech with tradition for a premium dining experience."

The room erupted in applause for Neil's presentation.

"You're a genius at merging tech with hospitality. This is definitely a modern dining experience," Aarav said.

"I have to say, I'm genuinely impressed, Neil. It's not every day I feel this way about you," a surprised voice chimed in. "Thank you, Milady," Neil responded, a little flustered.

"What was that, Neil? Did you say something?" Rishi asked playfully.

"Nothing, just expressing gratitude," Neil replied, recovering quickly.

"Rishi, it's your turn now," Aarav passed the baton.

"Thanks, Neil! Great presentation, by the way. Now, let me introduce the 'Ambrosia' and 'Kessanet' apps, your go-to for everything related to our restaurants.

Starting with the Ambrosia app, available in the App Store, users can create an account to book tables. It functions like a movie ticket booking app, showing available tables based on reservations. Ambrosia operates on a booking-slot system—no walk-ins allowed. If a slot is empty, a staff member will be at the door to assist with real-time availability updates for last-minute cancellations. Once you book a slot, just show your phone to the doorman, who will update your table status. A notification will go to your assigned waiter, so they can assist you right away.

There's also a tutorial in the app to guide you through the booking process. Customer data will be tracked so users can monitor their visit history, and the app supports online payments.

Next up is the Kessanet app, which has a slightly different approach. Here, you book at the door. After logging into the app, simply tell the door attendant your Customer ID, and they'll mark your status. You can then see available tables and book one accordingly. Once seated, your name will be displayed at your assigned table, and the tablet there will automatically log you in for easy ordering.

The app also includes a 'Kessanet Special' for booking the gaming zone or theater based on available slots. If you select a film, you'll see various options and can search for specific titles. Just like at a theater, your show will be booked automatically. You can also choose from various food and beverage combos. Note: no outside snacks allowed; the theater has a standard package you can customize.

One more thing: there are no discounts or coupons for Ambrosia, but frequent visitors will have their customer badge upgraded. Once you reach the platinum level, you get a free visit! Plus, you'll have priority booking preferences. Ambrosia essentially has a loyalty program."

The room filled with cheers and applause for Rishi's presentation.

"Great job, champ!" Aarav praised. "Amazing work, Rishi," Neil added. "You're really impressive," Shabby complimented.

"I pass the baton to our final presenter, Aarav," Rishi said.

"Thanks, Rishi! Fantastic job in such a short time. Now, for the launch of the year: Ambrosia and Kessanet! Let's give a loud round of applause to our quiet manager, Joe, for successfully convincing Chef Koel to feature his finest dishes on our menu!"

The room erupted in applause.

"You may not say much, but you always get the job done. Great skills, Joe," Aarav acknowledged. "Thanks, Aarav and everyone."

"Next up, my buddy and partner in crime, Sri! You've done an amazing job training our staff to the highest standards. Let's hear it for Sri!"

"Thanks, everyone. Aarav, I appreciate your trust in me," Sri replied warmly.

"Alright, let's get back to tomorrow's event. As Neil mentioned, we kick off at 8 PM. Our group stakeholders and their families are our first guests, and their logins are already set in our apps. This launch is crucial for our expansion plans; if they believe in our concept, we'll be well-positioned for fundraising.

Mr. Ahuja, Neil's father, will be our Chief Guest for the ribbon-cutting ceremony, which will also be covered by the media. This stakeholder experience is our first litmus test. If we succeed here, we'll be ready for our customers.

We've got everything lined up, but this meeting is about addressing any last-minute details. Team, we have a lot riding on this project. Let's deliver our best and trust the process. Stay calm—even if something goes awry, handle it with poise and experience.

Are we ready to take on the world and show them what we can do?"

"Yes!" the team shouted in unison.

"Let's do this! I need to find us a piano artist, so go home, rest up, and we'll meet tomorrow."

As Aarav left, he decided to visit an old friend.

"Can I come in?" Aarav asked as he entered. "It's been a while since we last met."

"Yes, Ryan, it's been too long! Are you still working as a waiter?" Aarav inquired.

"Hey, not everyone is as talented and resourceful as you. I have to work harder if I want to make something of myself," Ryan replied.

"Aarav, you have immense potential, and you know it!" Ryan encouraged.

"Seriously? You really think so?" Aarav asked, surprised.

"Absolutely. Your heart is good, Aarav. Most people wouldn't maintain a friendship with someone who once worked as their helper," Ryan reassured him.

"No, I took that job because I wanted to earn my course fee, which you were already offering as a loan. I wasn't sure if I could repay you, so I thought I'd work instead," Aarav confessed.

"I knew you never wanted the money back," Ryan said with a smile. "Your intentions were pure. Now it's my time to return the favor."

"Return the favor? How?" Ryan questioned.

"By making you happy," Aarav replied.

"I am happy, Aarav. Why would you think otherwise?" Ryan asked.

"Because I haven't seen you play the piano in years," Aarav remarked.

"It's been a while," Ryan admitted. "Honestly, I stopped playing because of what happened with her. You know, when we were young, we all get swept up in fantasies. I was the 'cool kid' because I could play, and that attracted her. But when college ended, the reality hit her. She thought I wasn't worth it. It's ironic how what we valued in college suddenly becomes unimportant once we enter the real world."

"You fell into the trap of trying to impress people who don't truly matter. I don't judge her choices, but if you're hurt, that's valid. But Ryan, when you played, your music had such depth. Don't let anyone's opinion make you abandon what you love," Aarav urged.

"You're right. Music used to bring me joy," Ryan admitted. "My father got me that piano because he wanted me to be happy. True love means wanting others to pursue what brings them joy. I know he would be heartbroken to see me like this."

"Enough of trying to prove your worth. Do what you love. Make your father proud," Aarav said sincerely. "Tomorrow, we're launching a new restaurant, and I promised to bring in the best piano artist. Here's my contact info. If you feel it's worth it, show up."

Launch Day

"What's the status of our guests, Neil?" Aarav asked.

"They'll arrive in half an hour," Joe replied.

"Perfect! We're all set, then," Neil said, looking pleased. "Joe?"

"Yes, Neil?"

"Quick recap of the schedule?"

"We'll kick off with the ribbon-cutting ceremony, followed by tours of both restaurants, and then a regular dinner service. We'll wrap up the day with a short team meeting to strategize for our official opening tomorrow."

"Rishi, are we ready on the app side?" Neil inquired.

"Absolutely, Neil. We're all set. Your dad will place the first order to kick things off, and we'll keep the launch reels and posts rolling out. We have the hotel tech team helping with all of this, right?"

"Yes, all the resources you allocated are in place, and the instructions are clear," Rishi confirmed.

"Great work, Rishi. Where's our COO?"

"No idea, Neil. Haven't seen him around," Joe replied.

"Did I hear 'COO'?" Aarav interjected, strolling in.

"Yes, Aarav, we were just talking about you," Neil said.

"Good! You thought of me. I'm here," Aarav grinned.

"You've got all the updates, right, Neil?"

"Yes, but there's one thing—what's the update on the piano?"

"Just a sec; I got a call," Neil said.

"Hey, Ryan! Is that you?" Aarav answered the phone. "Yes, you've got the right location. Timing couldn't be better—we were just discussing the piano artist!"

"Aarav, first off, that speech you gave last night was way too boring and dragged on. If you had just asked me to play, I would've jumped at the chance," Ryan teased.

"I'll take that feedback onboard for next time," Aarav laughed.

"This place is incredible, Aarav! It feels like a palace!" Ryan exclaimed.

"Team, this is Ryan, our piano artist," Aarav introduced him. "Ryan, meet Neil."

"Hi, Ryan. Welcome aboard!" Neil greeted.

"Thanks, Neil. So we're all set for the launch?" Ryan asked.

"Where's Shabby?" Aarav wondered.

"I'm not sure, but she said she was on her way," Neil replied just as Shabby entered.

"Here I am, Mr. CEO!" she announced. Everyone gasped at her stunning black gown.

"Wow, you look incredible, Shabby," Neil said, taken aback.

"Thanks! So, you were looking for me?" she asked, eyeing Aarav.

"No, I just wanted to say you look stunning," Aarav corrected.

"Did I ask you what I look like, Mr. CEO?" Shabby quipped, a playful smirk on her face.

"Not my fault; it was spontaneous!" Neil interjected.

"Keep your comments in check, Mr. CEO," she joked.

"Looks like you'll steal the spotlight today, Shabby. The restaurant might just be secondary," Aarav teased.

"Thanks, Aarav," she replied, smiling.

"Guys, guests are gathering outside Ambrosia. It's time to get this show on the road!" Joe announced.

"Hi, Dad! You've been so curious about what I've been up to—now you'll see it firsthand," Neil said excitedly.

"Ladies and gentlemen, I'm Neil Ahuja, and on behalf of my team, I welcome you to the launch of our two new restaurants!" The guests looked surprised.

"Two restaurants?" his father asked, astonished.

"Yes, Dad! Now let's cut this ribbon and officially inaugurate them!"

With that, Mr. Ahuja cut the ribbon, and the crowd erupted in applause. "Ladies and gentlemen, I present to you Ambrosia and Kessanet—our modern flagship restaurants!"

"Come on in; this is our premium restaurant, Ambrosia." Mr. Ahuja's eyes lit up as he entered. He was in awe of the elegant setup.

"Please place the first order from your table to kick off our app!" Neil encouraged.

"How did you manage all this in such a short time, son?" Mr. Ahuja asked, genuinely impressed.

"I have the best team by my side, Dad," Neil replied proudly.

"This looks better than many hotel restaurants. I can't believe I'm sitting in an Indian restaurant; it feels so upscale. I'm beyond proud of you, son!" Mr. Ahuja said, becoming emotional.

"Now, please make an order and see how everything works," Neil urged.

The guests enjoyed their meals, marveling at everything Ambrosia and Kessanet had to offer.

"Attention, everyone! It's time for our piano artist, Ryan, to perform. His music will be a key part of Ambrosia's charm," Neil announced as guests explored the restaurant.

As Ryan began to play "What's Between Us," the atmosphere turned magical.

"Aarav, this piece is incredible! It's been so long since I've experienced such a deep performance. Now I understand why you insisted on having Ryan—his music adds an entirely new dimension to our restaurant," Neil remarked.

"Thanks, Neil! Just look at our stakeholders; their reactions speak volumes. Chef Koel's menu is getting the most orders! And over at Kessanet, our stakeholders are watching a movie with their families. Their engagement says it all."

"Aarav, I'm thrilled to see my father so happy. He's finally witnessing something he always dreamed of doing," Neil said, his eyes shining.

"Yes, we may have the best restaurant, but running a successful business is a whole different challenge. Tomorrow we go live, and then we'll really find out if this is a success or not," Neil reminded him.

"But for today, let's celebrate what we've built!"

Everyone enjoyed themselves as Neil introduced his father to the team, sharing stories of their journey. He made a special introduction for Shabby, and Mr. Ahuja noticed the chemistry between them.

Now, they were entering the true test phase—the real litmus test from the customers. The excitement of what was to come hung in the air as they looked forward to the journey ahead.

Time Jump: Eight Months Later

"Mr. Aggarwal, I've already mentioned that all the stats, reports, and our expansion plan will be unveiled at the AGM tomorrow. I understand the board members' excitement, but I believe it's only fair to wait just one more day," Neil said, maintaining a professional tone.

"We're eagerly anticipating the AGM," a board member chimed in.

"Aarav, have you gone through the entire presentation prepared by Rishi?" Neil asked.

"Yes, Neil, I reviewed it thoroughly," Aarav replied.

"Good. However, there's going to be a change in our previous plan," Neil said, pausing for a moment.

"What do you mean?" Aarav asked, curious.

"Instead of me presenting, I'm going to ask you to take the lead on the presentation," Neil stated.

"Why me?" Aarav asked, surprised.

"Because you've been the driving force behind it all, and you deserve the opportunity to showcase what we've accomplished over the past eight months," Neil explained.

"Thanks, Neil. That's really thoughtful of you," Aarav replied appreciatively.

"Honestly, it's more strategic than sentimental. I plan to get formal approval for your appointment as COO from the board, so it makes sense for you to present," Neil continued.

"Your wish is my command, Boss," Aarav smiled.

"Make sure you arrive on time for tomorrow's meeting, Mr. COO. Your reputation for punctuality has been a bit shaky," Neil joked.

"Who told you that?" Aarav asked.

"You might be surprised to learn that it's the HR department. Apparently, you've been late every single day for the past eight months," Neil chuckled.

"I don't know what to say in my defense. Mornings have never been my strong suit, or you could say that nights get the better of me," Aarav confessed.

"Enough with the excuses, Aarav. I'll give you one word: lazy. You're lazy, and that's the end of the story," Neil stated matter-of-factly.

"That's exactly what I was trying to avoid, but I guess you're too smart for that," Aarav retorted.

"Yes, I am smart, and you are lazy. I think once is enough; no need to keep repeating it. I promise I'll be on time tomorrow," Aarav assured.

"Did you check in with Joe, Ryan, and Shabby about how they're managing the restaurants? Especially with Sri and the grooming department?" Neil asked.

"Yes, I've been monitoring everything since we started preparing for the AGM," Aarav confirmed.

"Good to hear. But let me tell you, Sri has gone a bit mad since we made him Head of the Grooming and Service department. It seems he's forgotten he has a brother named Aarav," Neil laughed.

"Shut up, Aarav. Sri's dedication ensures our service standards remain high. He's very reliable," Neil replied.

"Alright, if you say so, Boss. Let's get some sleep; tomorrow is crucial. Just one last thing: Rishi, be prepared with the entire presentation and setup," Aarav reminded.

"Got it, Aarav. I'll be ready," Rishi assured.

"Very good, Rishi. And please, try not to use the hotel swimming pool. Since we arrived, I've had complaints that you keep swimming even after the pool hours end," Aarav warned.

"You know I love the pool, Aarav," Rishi protested.

"I know, but just for tomorrow, please avoid it. I don't want any distractions during the AGM," Aarav instructed.

"Okay, okay! But once the AGM is over, I'll be diving back in with you and Neil," Rishi said.

"Count me in!" Neil chimed in.

"Now, let's get some rest. Tomorrow is an important day," Aarav concluded.

Annual General Meeting of Ahuja's Sons

"Welcome, everyone, to the Annual General Meeting of Ahuja's Sons. Today's meeting is crucial as we will present detailed reports on our recent ventures, Ambrosia and Kessanet. We also have some announcements regarding our future plans, particularly for our media friends who have been curious about our direction in recent months," Neil began.

"I'd like to invite Aarav, the COO of the Ambrosia and Kessanet restaurant chain in the NCR region, to present to the board," he continued.

"Thank you, Neil. Hello, everyone, I'm Aarav. The past eight months have been remarkable for our company since launching Ambrosia and Kessanet. When comparing the performance of our hotels and restaurants, it's evident that the Ambrosia and Kessanet chain, consisting of seven restaurants, has generated nearly 800 crores in revenue—our highest achievement to date. In contrast, our hotels only managed to bring in 500 crores, marking their lowest performance in recent years, despite having ten hotels with a revenue period of 12 months. Ambrosia and Kessanet, however, accomplished this in just eight months," Aarav reported.

"The revenue generated by a single restaurant in just one month has been staggering, leading us to open six more within two months. The entire team has worked tirelessly to ensure this rapid rollout. Our success with Ambrosia and Kessanet demonstrates that it's time to rethink traditional restaurant operations," he emphasized.

"Can you share the profit margins for Ambrosia and Kessanet individually?" Mr. Aggarwal asked.

"Certainly, Mr. Aggarwal. Ambrosia has a profit margin of 25%, while Kessanet boasts an impressive 45%," Aarav explained.

"Forty-five percent? That's incredible!" Mr. Aggarwal exclaimed, surprised.

"Yes, sir, 45%. The concept of designing two products within a single setup has yielded unexpected rewards," Aarav replied.

"I've personally experienced the demand; my sons' reservations were denied at Kessanet Theatre, so I understand the buzz surrounding it. The Ambrosia and Kessanet app has surpassed 10 million downloads in just eight months, which speaks volumes," Mr. Ahuja added.

"After deducting operating and one-time setup costs for all seven restaurants, the net profit for the chain stands at 206 crores. This makes Ambrosia and Kessanet financially independent of Ahuja's Sons' funding," Aarav stated.

"I'm receiving daily calls from friends and family struggling to make reservations, which reflects the tremendous buzz around our brand," Mr. Ahuja remarked.

"Now that we know the product is a hit, Neil and I have agreed that it's time to introduce our concept nationwide, targeting major cities across every state with a total of 50 restaurants featuring both Ambrosia and Kessanet," Aarav continued.

"However, we wish to establish a separate firm to oversee the Ambrosia and Kessanet business. Ahuja's Sons will focus solely on hotels. We are pleased to introduce the new firm, which has been approved by major stakeholders, including Mr. Ahuja, who holds 70% ownership."

"This new entity will be called the Privisha Group, a name inspired by Neil Ahuja's parents, the late Mrs. Prisha Ahuja and Mr. Vihaan Ahuja. It's essential for the growth of Ambrosia and Kessanet to separate it from Ahuja's Sons," Aarav explained.

"The Privisha Group will exclusively focus on expanding the Ambrosia and Kessanet chain throughout the country. Opening 50 restaurants is no small feat, particularly financially. Therefore, we are offering 10% equity to stakeholders for an investment of 500 crores, with an initial valuation of 5000 crores."

"We aim to target an IPO in two years, diluting 30% of the holdings. As board members of Ahuja's Sons, this offer is a privilege; we intend to bypass another funding round and instead aim for an IPO launch after achieving our target of 4000 crores in post-capital," Aarav concluded.

"Your valuation seems ambitious, considering this comes just eight months after launching. I know from experience that the novelty of a product can fade over time," Mr. Sejwal interjected.

"I appreciate your perspective, Mr. Sejwal. The restaurant business is driven by innovation. If we don't update our offerings regularly, we risk losing market share. That's why it's crucial for us to consistently innovate and improve," Aarav responded.

"Regarding our success in other states, I can't guarantee it will be the same as in NCR. When we started, we had no idea if it would work, but we took the risk, which is a fundamental aspect of business," Aarav elaborated.

"We plan to leverage technology in our marketing to ensure our products become local highlights. We're identifying prime locations and collecting market data. Each restaurant will be designed based on the slogan 'one state, one theme,' giving each state a unique identity," Aarav explained enthusiastically.

"That's an interesting approach, Aarav. I also believe, Mr. Sejwal, that it's time to revolutionize the way restaurants operate in this country, and we can be the pioneers of that change. The demand for quality dining experiences is clear across the nation," Mr. Ahuja added.

"Based on the current performance, each restaurant is generating about 5 crores monthly, which translates to a potential profit of 3000 crores. Even accounting for various factors, I can see a profit of at least 2000 crores in a calendar year, making me interested in investing," Mr. Aggarwal expressed.

"I'd like to take 5% equity, as well as Mr. Oberoi, who is also interested in a 5% stake," he announced.

The AGM concluded, covering various aspects of the business, including the hotel chain.

"That went well, Aarav," Neil said, pleased. "I could see the board's reactions when we introduced the Privisha Group idea. Our business's selling point is exceeding expectations in every area, including stakeholder satisfaction."

"With the investment approved, we're ready to launch the restaurant chain nationwide, focusing on the next step: the expansion phase," Aarav confirmed.

"Today, Ahuja's Sons has announced the formation of the Privisha Group, which will manage the Ambrosia and Kessanet chains across the country. We will be launching 50 restaurants in key locations over the coming months. This update is significant for the food and service industry, as Ambrosia and Kessanet have generated considerable buzz in the northern region," the news anchor announced.

"During the AGM, it was revealed that the chain achieved an impressive 800 crores in revenue in just eight months. This is promising for the Ahuja Group, especially after a challenging few years. With Ambrosia and Kessanet, they hope to reach new heights in the service sector," she continued.

"The turnaround credit goes to the dynamic duo, Neil Ahuja, CEO, and Aarav, COO of the new entity. Our correspondent had a chance to speak with them post-AGM. Let's hear their thoughts," she said.

"Shivanya? Come here!" Maya called out.

"What is it, Maya? Why are you shouting?" Shivanya responded.

"Remember that guy who spilled a drink on you at that event? What about him?" Maya asked.

"Did he do something wrong again?" Shivanya questioned, puzzled.

"Just look at the TV!" Maya pointed.

"I'm joined by CEO Neil and COO Aarav. First of all, congratulations on your success with Ambrosia and Kessanet; it has truly transformed the service sector. Thank you! We're thrilled to provide our customers with the best products," Neil said.

"There's a lot of excitement about your recent expansion plans discussed at the AGM. We have significant offerings for customers on a national level," Aarav added.

"Mr. Aarav, you seem to be an unexpected topic of discussion. Can you tell us how you achieved this success and how you ended up partnering with Neil?" the interviewer asked.

"My journey with Neil began simply; I was a waiter in the same chain, and he recognized my potential and took a chance on me. The rest is history," Aarav explained.

"As for the product idea, it's a collaborative effort led by our entire team, with Neil at the helm," Aarav concluded.

You've accomplished something quite remarkable, Aarav. Can you share what motivated you to reach this point? I believe the journey is still ongoing, and I haven't done anything extraordinary that hasn't been done before. Sometimes, you need a catalyst, a person who can inspire or push you to break through your limits. I find that the best motivator is when someone helps you see your true potential in this vast world.

Who would that person be for you, Mr. Aarav? That's a bit personal, so I prefer not to disclose their identity. It's less about who they are and more about how you react when faced with that eye-opening moment.

Congratulations again to both of you on your success, and best wishes for your upcoming projects. Thank you!

Did you just see that, Maya? It's hard to believe. That guy is now the COO of the fastest-growing restaurant chain in the northern region. I'm not sure how to process this. And he was talking about me? It appears to be true, Shivanya.

How dare he? Even if he successfully opens these restaurants, how can he mention me like that? Well, he didn't directly mention you; it's just our speculation.

No, Maya, I know exactly who he was referring to. What's with Neil making some random guy the COO of his company? I did some digging when I visited Ambrosia last month, Shivanya. Ambrosia is, without a doubt, the best place out there.

Tell me about your findings, Maya. I've heard plenty about Ambrosia. Yes, Shivanya, the entire concept of creating the two restaurants, Ambrosia and Kessanet, was Aarav's idea. People familiar with the daily operations say Aarav has a sharp mind that's quite rare these days.

A sharp mind? Yes, Shivanya. I've seen many sharp minds come and go, and I doubt he'll be any different. He'll struggle as the business grows because managing a service business on a large scale is extremely challenging.

Why are you reacting this way? Why let him affect you? Is something bothering you, Shivanya? No, Maya, do you really think I'd be affected by him? I couldn't care less if he makes it or not. I'm merely sharing my thoughts on how these businesses operate.

Aarav, the COO of the Privisha Group. So, it's official; he's the COO now. I can see it on the company website. The news is true, Shivanya.

Forget all of that, Maya. Lakshya invited me to dinner tomorrow, and guess what? It's in Ambrosia. I'm excited to see what all the fuss is about.

Sri, I've finished with the AGM. Have you arranged everything? Yes, Aarav, it's all set. You just need to pick up Uncle Param. Great, I'll grab him right now and send you a text.

Okay, Aarav. Got it.

Uncle Param, how are you? I'm doing well, Aarav. It's been a long time since I last saw you. Have you been busy with work? Yes, uncle, I've just been caught up with some tasks. Son, I got a bit emotional the other day and said a lot of things. Don't worry about the house; it's not your responsibility.

Do you really think so, Uncle? Even if I wanted to, I couldn't get you 3 crores in one year. Yes, son, I know that's nearly impossible for you.

It is impossible, but one thing is definitely possible: we can go for an outing together. An outing? Yes, Uncle, I have a surprise planned for you. I'll blindfold you, and we'll drive there. Son, why are you doing all this? Don't worry; it'll be fun!

We've arrived at the destination, Uncle. Let me help you out. Walk slowly; we're almost there. Now it's time to unveil your blindfold. Are you ready for the surprise? Yes, son, let's see it. Surprise! Everyone shouted. Welcome home, Uncle Param!

Aarya, my girl, when did you arrive? I came to surprise you. Aarav told me he renovated our property to surprise you with this new home. Look at our home, father! It's beautiful, and I never imagined Aarav would surprise us like this.

Aarav, how did you manage all of this? Uncle, there's a saying that if you're committed to a purpose, the universe helps you achieve it in every way. Now let's not waste time, Uncle. Step into your new home and inaugurate it.

Aarav, my son. Your eyes say it all. The joy I see in your eyes is fulfilling in every way. Everyone thoroughly enjoyed the inauguration ceremony.

Sri, we need to head out now. Tomorrow, our expansion program begins, and we have a lot to prepare. Yes, Aarav, I'm coming.

Aarav, my son. Yes, Uncle Param? Where are you going? Back to work, Uncle. Wait! First, tell me how you pulled this off. Forget about saving the house; you've renovated it beautifully. Uncle, you need to know that Aarav is now the COO of a renowned restaurant company. He bought this home three months ago and renovated it. What are you saying, Sri? My Aarav is the COO of a company? Yes, Uncle, it's true.

Uncle Param, don't worry about how I did this. What matters is that I was able to do it in time. I couldn't bear to see my parents lose their home.

Aarav, my son, no one does what you've done for us. I don't know if we treated you like a son, but you've certainly treated us like your parents. Uncle, please don't say that; you've given me everything. Offering a place in your home to this homeless orphan means more than anything I've done.

Now, let go of your worries and enjoy life. Also, Aarya knows nothing about any of this, so it's a secret between us.

I bless you, my son, and Laxmi in heaven will do the same. You will achieve whatever you want because you have what it takes to succeed.

Thank you, Uncle. That was more than I could have hoped for. I'll certainly do my best. Okay, take care and try to enjoy yourself a bit.

On the way back home. Aarav, it still feels surreal that you saved the house. Sri, we live in a world where few truly understand the meaning of life. Life is about finding your path and moving forward until you reach a point where you can pass the baton.

So, this achievement is just one goal in our ongoing journey.

We may have passed a significant test, but reaching the heights I aspire to is still a challenge. Let's see what the future holds for me.

Target- IPO and AVCL launch

Isn't this place amazing, Shivanya? Absolutely, Lakshya! Ambrosia truly exudes elegance and definitely meets our high standards. Did you know that Neil Ahuja owns this place? Ahuja Uncle's son? Really? I'm thrilled for Ahuja Uncle; he's always dreamt of creating something like this.

But I've heard, Shivanya, that Neil has cut ties with the Sen family, despite your father and Uncle Ahuja being childhood friends. This all started when Dad bought stakes in a rival hotel company, Lakshya. Neil was understandably upset by that move. Ahuja's family faced significant financial losses, going from market leaders in the northern region to the very bottom. They managed to bounce back, but things were never quite the same.

You know how particular Dad is about business. He believes in keeping family and business separate, and I think that affected our relationship with Neil. Ahuja Uncle thought Shaurya made that decision, and he couldn't let friendship interfere with business. But Neil didn't take it well.

Neil and I were like siblings growing up, but everything changed when I went abroad for my studies. It's been ages since we last spoke.

Don't feel bad, Shivanya. This isn't your fault or your father's. I believe Neil would understand. Your dad's decision was strictly a business one and had nothing to do with his friendship with Ahuja Uncle.

Hey, Sri! What's up? You know who we're hosting today at our Ambrosia main branch? Who? Shivanya Sen and her fiancé, Lakshya Seth. No way! You must be joking. I'm not joking!

I should inform Mr. COO about this. He'll definitely want to know.

Aarav! Yes, Sri? What's going on? Do you know who we're hosting today? Who? Your dream girl. No way, she's not coming here. Actually, it looks like she is. Are you serious, Sri? Yes, Aarav. And let me guess, Lakshya will be with her. Yes, Mr. Lover Boy! Hey, I'm not a lover boy!

So, has Ryan performed yet? No, he'll be on in about five minutes. Okay, Ryan bro, this is Aarav. Yeah, what's up? Can you play a piece that creates romantic tension? Why's that? I'll explain later.

Got it, Aarav.

Seriously, what's this romantic tension you keep talking about? Sri, it's a feeling only those involved truly understand. But how do you know she's even involved? Sri, I can sense there's tension between us. No, there's no tension! Stop imagining a fantasy that'll never come true.

You want to see the tension, Sri? I'm not interested in your love story. I've got too much work to do, so I'm leaving you to handle it.

Aarav stepped into the lobby of Ambrosia after coming from the office. He spotted Shivanya for the first time in eight months.

Aarav, why are you just standing there? Need something? No, Joe, I'm just admiring the most beautiful sight in the world. What are you talking about? Never mind, Joe. I'm heading to the main area to see how everything is running.

Okay, Aarav, but why the sudden inspection? Not an inspection, Joe. Just relax and make sure our guests are enjoying themselves. Got it, Aarav!

Ryan began playing a piece called "Are You Still There for Me."

Shivanya, do you want anything? No, Lakshya, I'm good. Then why are you looking around as if you're searching for something? I'm just admiring the design of the place, that's all.

Suddenly, Shivanya noticed Aarav at the reception. When their eyes met, it felt like time froze until the piano music ended.

After the performance, Shivanya and Lakshya prepared to leave the restaurant.

Waiting for your car? Yes. Where's your partner? He's coming from the restroom. Aarav, right? If I recall correctly? Yes, that's me. Why were you looking at me earlier? I could ask you the same thing. Aarav, it's rude; I told you before. My bad, Shivanya. I'll be more careful next time.

If you think there's something between us, let me warn you: don't dream of anything impossible, at least not in this lifetime. I don't dream. One question though: how many years are left? Too many, Aarav, and you won't be able to bridge that gap.

What really matters, Shivanya, is whether you want me to close that gap. It doesn't matter what I want, Aarav; it's simply not going to happen. So, just stay away from me.

Actually, you're the one who came to my place if we're being logical here. Whatever, Aarav, just stay away from me. You didn't just show up here randomly. I know you knew I'd be here, didn't you?

You think too much, Aarav. And I can't believe you're not afraid of anything. Do you know who I am? I'm Shivanya Sen, daughter of India's biggest industrialist. Are you saying that to me or convincing yourself, Shivanya? What do you mean?

I mean you're trying to convince yourself that you can't fall for a regular guy just because of your family name. You're a disgusting man, Mr. Aarav. And you're a beautiful woman, Ms. Shivanya Sen. Take care, and don't dwell on me too much. Now, I need to go before that Mr. CEO Emilink shows up and bombards us with unnecessary questions.

Aarav, I'll kill you for this! Bye, Shivanya, take care!

How did our AGM go, Mr. CEO?

It was fantastic, Shabby! We successfully raised the funds we need for our expansion plan.

Great, Neil! But what's the plan for expansion?

What's on your mind, Shabby?

Nothing, just joking!

Alright, team, we need to replicate our business model on a national level now. It won't be easy due to the sheer scale involved, but we're gearing up for the challenge by expanding our teams. For the next month, we'll focus on deploying our resources in the field. Shabby's team will handle the design for each restaurant chain, while Joe's team will take care of developing the spaces. Sri, your team will oversee training our staff on a large scale—we've even acquired a facility for this purpose. Rishi, Aarav, and I will manage marketing, tech, and strategy for our nationwide operations.

In the first phase, Shabby and Joe's teams will be at the forefront since you'll need to complete the restaurant builds on time. Then Sri's team will allocate human resources for each location. Finally, my team will handle the chain launch and all branding aspects.

Joe?

Yes, Neil?

I think we'll need a VP of Ground Development for this nationwide restaurant building effort.

Absolutely, you'll need someone to oversee my team's progress.

Aarav, do you have anyone in mind for the VP role?

I do, Neil! I have a letter stating that Mr. Joe is being promoted to VP of Ground Development at The Privisha Group.

Joe was filled with joy.

Congratulations, Joe! You absolutely deserve this!

Thanks, Shabby! Neil, I'm thrilled for this opportunity.

You've earned it, Joe. Now, go celebrate—take a day off and spend time with your family!

Thanks, Neil, and thanks to the entire team for your support!

Alright, team, in two months, we'll be deploying restaurants nationwide, so let's stick to our timelines. Meeting dismissed.

TWO YEARS LATER

Neil's team has worked tirelessly for two years to build The Privisha Group, and now it's time for the IPO listing day. The response has been overwhelming, with the IPO being oversubscribed by about 180 times.

IPO Listing Day

What do you think, Aarav? What will our listing price be?
Definitely above the offered price of 120 Rs/share, Neil. I think it'll hit 180.
You guys don't get business—at 180 times oversubscription, we'll be opening between 200 and 250.
Shabby, you're being too optimistic.
I'm not being overly optimistic, Mr. CEO; the numbers back me up.

We're gearing up, team, to see our hard work pay off. I want you all to know how grateful I am for everything you've helped me achieve. With today's IPO listing, I'll fulfill my mother's dream of seeing our company listed on the stock market—she always believed I could do it.
Thank you for your support, everyone.
Neil, this journey has been a collective achievement, as Aarav pointed out.

Guys, it's listing time! I'm excited to witness this! The Privisha Group's IPO listed at 206 Rs/share, and the announcement was made.
Yessssss! The entire team erupted in joy and excitement. Emotions were running high as they celebrated their incredible achievement together.

We're joined by The Privisha Group team on their IPO listing day: Mr. CEO Neil Ahuja, COO Aarav, Chief Designer Shabby, VP of Training Sri, VP of Tech Rishi, and VP of Ground Development Joe.

First off, congratulations to the entire team on this massive success, the media anchor said.
Thank you, madam, Neil replied.

I'd like to know, Neil, what do you believe is the reason behind the success of the Ambrosia and Kessanet chains?
When you have the right team, strategy, product, and execution, you achieve what Ambrosia and Kessanet have. We managed to navigate the challenges of expansion smoothly because we knew exactly what we wanted to do. If you know your product fits the market, implementing it at a broader scale becomes much easier.

Neil, I have another question: how did you manage to get everything right? It's tough to nail it all in one go.
I admit, getting everything right is challenging. But it doesn't happen by chance; it takes a lot of hard work to make things fall into place. Landing on the right path requires extensive background efforts.

I've gotten insights into what makes Ambrosia and Kessanet so appealing. The concept of combining premium and casual gatherings in one location is revolutionary. The way it's implemented is key to its success. They've also highlighted the tech advancements at both restaurants, and overall, their social media presence is doing wonders. They've given a lot of credit to the design team for creating such beautiful spaces across the country.
Well, when it comes to the idea, it was Aarav's concept to offer something like this, and the design was brought to life by the one and only Shabby Arora, Neil said.

Shabby, I'm a big fan of your work! Can you share how you came up with these stunning themes for the restaurants?
It was my first and biggest challenge due to the scale of the project. Visualizing the space in a particular way is crucial when designing. Ambrosia's design is inspired by a premium space set

against a natural backdrop, giving that fresh feeling we experience in nature. Kessanet, on the other hand, captures a cool vibe of modern times.

The theme ideas were pretty spontaneous—just how I envisioned a premium place would look if I were to visit one.

Now, on the operational side, Joe, how do you manage logistics?

Logistics is crucial in the service sector, especially if you want to stay ahead of competitors. For our nationwide operations, we partnered with local vendors for raw materials for food and beverages. Our specialty is our quality checks on these materials, which allows us to serve quality food to our customers. This strategic local partnership is essential in building this empire. We've set up regional branches in each state to manage everything from payments to vendor interactions, allowing local vendors to coordinate effectively and receive timely payments.

Lastly, I want to bring up Mr. Aarav. I've noticed you've been avoiding the limelight. How did you come up with this idea?

I wasn't hiding; I just wanted my teammates to take the spotlight. As for the idea, sure, you can think of creative concepts, but unless you back them up with the right strategy and execution, they're worthless. Creative thinking alone isn't enough.

It's been great catching up with The Privisha Group team. Congratulations again on your IPO listing!

This wraps up a significant chapter of our story. Now we move on to the next chapter centered around AVCL, but first, let's witness a marriage—let's dive right into it!

Shabby and Neil's Wedding Day

Do you realize how lucky you are, Mr. Neil Ahuja?

Not really, Ms. Shreya Arora, or should I say Mrs. Shreya Ahuja?

Honestly, I think I'm making a huge mistake marrying you.

Why's that, Shabby?

Because you don't care about me!

I've cared about you since the first time I saw you in school.

Yeah, I've heard that before.

You have to propose to me properly, or forget about marrying me.

Shabby, we're getting married today; we can do this later.

Nope! You'll propose to me right now, or nothing's happening!

Why are you suddenly acting like a silly girl?

Because it dawned on me that you never actually proposed; you just showed up at my door with your family to arrange this wedding!

Shreya, seriously?

Yes, Mr. CEO, do it now!

Alright, Mrs. Ahuja, here goes.

Neil dropped to one knee and said, "I was lost and had no one to support me, but when you came into my life, Shreya, I felt a joy I can't put into words. I've always dreamed of marrying you since our school days. I want you by my side until my last breath. I love you, Shreya Arora. Will you marry me?"

Say yes, Shreya—my knees are hurting!

Let them hurt, you idiot. I love you too; come here!

After that, the wedding rituals unfolded beautifully.

They look so happy, don't they?

Yes, they do! I'm happy for Neil.

What about me?

What about you, Lakshya?

Hello, Miss Shivanya, it's me, Aarav!

Not you again! By the way, Lakshya isn't invited, and you didn't come with him—just for your information.

Let me guess: it was your idea not to invite Lakshya to this wedding.

Yes, exactly! Why would I want someone bothering us while we're busy?

You and I busy with what?

Yes, Shivanya. I'm here because Neil is my childhood friend.

But he didn't invite you.

I know, but Uncle Ahuja did.

I see. It's been two years since we last met, and you thought this would be the perfect time to catch up with me, didn't you?

Not really, Mr. Aarav. By the way, why don't you have a last name?

Because I'm an orphan.

Oh, I'm sorry to hear that.

What do you want from me, Aarav?

Your time, Shivanya.

Don't look at me like that, Aarav.

Why not, Shivanya?

Aarav, why do you always push me like this? Tell me, did you miss me over the last two years?

Aarav, for your information, I'm getting engaged to Lakshya later this year.

Oh, I see you're getting engaged. So, you've agreed to marry Lakshya Seth?

It's already decided that I will marry Lakshya.

Don't tell me what's decided, Shivanya.

Did you agree to marry Lakshya?

Aarav, I don't feel like telling you this. You're nobody to me.

Why do you keep showing up in my life and creating chaos?

I told you before, we don't match.

I'm not asking if we're a match; I'm asking if you agreed to marry him.

I know you didn't, Shivanya. Don't act like you don't care where I've been and what I've done over the past two years. I know you've been keeping tabs on me since we last met. I know you celebrated my success.

That attitude you have doesn't come from a genuine place; you're lonely inside. No one has ever tried to understand what you truly feel or what you want to do.

How do I know? Because I feel a connection with you.

Do you feel that connection with Lakshya?

I know you're here because your heart pushed you to come meet me.

Aarav, how can you confront me like this? You have no right to ask those questions. Don't use your tricks on me.

I'm a serious person; I don't like to play games with you. And I'm not confronting you—I'm just speaking the truth.

The truth is, Aarav, I'm getting engaged to Lakshya, and that's final.

Okay, Shivanya, if that's what you say.

Where are you going, Aarav?

What now, Shivanya?

What do you want me to stay for? So you can show me how certain you are about marrying Lakshya?

You really don't have any manners, do you? When we're having a conversation, you can't just walk away!

Aarav smiled. Fine, Shivanya, I'm not going anywhere until we finish this talk.

Better!

Why are you like this, Aarav?

Like what?

Intriguing.

Well, when I see you, I kind of turn into this person, Shivanya.

Aarav and Shivanya engaged in captivating conversations throughout the wedding.

I'll be leaving now, Aarav.

Shivanya, at least meet Neil once!

No, Aarav, I don't want to spoil the moment. I've met Uncle Vihaan.

Okay, as you wish. I had a great time today; I don't remember the last time I talked so much with anyone.

Always my pleasure, Shivanya.

Shivanya?

What is it, Aarav? You're leaving me?

Please don't do this, Aarav.

No, I'm serious, Shivanya.

Aarav, I have to go!

Don't go, please!

Aarav, don't start this now—I really have to leave. And as for leaving you, think of it this way: earlier, it wasn't even a possibility, but now there's at least some hope.

You made my day, Shivanya.

Yes, you're right; I have hope that one day you'll stay.

You're too much, Aarav. Bye, and take care of everyone.

Bye, Shivanya. You take care too.

The wedding concludes, but the story of Aarav and Shivanya has taken an interesting turn. The question now is how Aarav can make Shivanya realize she's meant for him, and how he can stop her engagement in less than a year. Let's see how this story unfolds.

Neil?

What's up, Aarav? It's only been a week since I got married. What's so urgent that you're interrupting my honeymoon?

Sorry, Neil, but I'm really pressed for time.

Pressed for time for what?

Connect with me on a video call.

Alright, give me a sec.

Okay, I'm ready.

Listen carefully, Neil: I'm planning to start an asset management company, and I want you to be a promoter with full financial backing.

What? Where did this AMC idea come from all of a sudden?

It's not sudden, Neil; I've been planning this for a while. Now is the right time to implement it.

How exactly do you plan to do this? And what about our restaurant business?

You'll continue managing the restaurant, Neil. I'm just no longer the COO. It's at a point where it needs proper monitoring and management for a while.

As for the implementation of the AMC, don't worry about that—it's my business.

Alright, Aarav, but what do you need me to do?

I just need you to be a promoter so I can attract investors.

Aarav, we know plenty of people who would be willing to fund us.

Neil, those people aren't AMC investors.

In exchange for 1,000 crores, I'll give you 10% stakes in the company.

10% for 1,000 crores? That's a big ask!

You're talking about stakes in an AMC. What do you think the scale of this firm will be?

It's going to be huge; otherwise, you wouldn't be interested.

Alright, you've got access to my funds, and my name as a promoter. I'll send you the documents—just sign them.

What's the name of the company?

It's called Asset Ventures Capital Limited, or AVCL.

Thumbs up! That's a cool name, Aarav. Your investment will diversify your portfolio, which will be helpful if you need funds for other business ventures in the future.

I see your point, Aarav. Honestly, I always knew once our restaurant business stabilized, you'd be off doing something else.

How do you know that?

Because you're an ambitious guy with a broad vision. You won't settle for anything less.

You know why I like you, Neil? Because you understand me. Best of luck, Aarav, and make sure my funds are safe.

Yes, Neil, I'll ensure that. Now I need to find a new COO.

In your case, Neil, you have a life partner who could easily become your business partner—I think you get my hint.

Got it, Mr. Aarav. Now go get to work!

Yes, Neil, and thanks again.

In a dramatic turn of events, the COO of The Privisha Group, Mr. Aarav, has launched an AMC firm, AVCL, and will be replaced by Shabby as COO. It seems like not everything is going smoothly at The Privisha Group, though, as it's rumored that AVCL is backed by CEO Neil. This sudden shift by Aarav raises questions. That's all for today's News Hour. Stay tuned for the latest updates.

You saw what's making the news, Aarav?

Yes, Sri, I heard. Let it be. I want everyone focused on the rift angle while I concentrate on AVCL.

So, what's the plan? You've started an AMC, but what's next?

Sri, don't worry too much about AVCL; just focus on your work.

I'm not worried; I don't do anything illegal or unethical. If I start an AMC, I'll run it with the highest business standards.

I have full faith in you, Aarav.

I know who's fueling this.

Who?

Shivanya Sen.

Sri, don't say such things so bluntly—be a little dramatic! You like her, don't you?

Sri, there are only two things I love in this world: Shivanya and technology.

I knew about the tech part but wasn't aware of the first one.

I have to go; I have a lot on my plate.

At the AVCL headquarters…

Rishi, is your team ready with those HFAs (High-Frequency Algorithms)?

Yes, almost done, Aarav.

When can I see them?

I'll be able to present them by tomorrow at the latest.

Okay, I'm locking in for tomorrow, but no further delays, Rishi—you know we need time to ensure these algorithms stabilize in the real market. I also want your team to clearly outline the differences between stock and crypto market HFAs.

Yes, Aarav, we've designed different HFAs for both markets.

Great! Tomorrow is your day, Rishi. Trust me, if this pays off, you could open your own gaming firm.

Surely, it will, Aarav. That's the spirit!

Now I need to meet someone; I'm looking for a personal assistant and financial advisor. In this new office, I'm surrounded by tech geeks, and I'm at the top of that list. I need someone with experience to give me a different perspective.

Where will you find that person, Aarav?

Rishi, I'll find them—just prepare for tomorrow.

Excuse me, one tea, please!

I have to say, roadside tea sellers are the best at making tea.

Thank you, bro, this tastes like heaven—so good! Have you seen Sharma Ji? He'll be here in 30 minutes.

How do you know?

He's retired from the stock market, but the stockbroker in him always brings him to this place we call the headquarters of the Indian stock market.

He'll come, sip some tea, catch up on the market updates with everyone around, and then head home. Classic Sharma Ji behavior!

After 1 Hour……

Hey, Sukesh, one tea, please.

What happened, Sharma Ji? You're late today!

Sukesh got stuck with some work at home.

Sharma Ji, who are you?

Aarav Ji! What a surprise to see you here!

I figured this was the only place I'd find you.

You know, the stock market is a place you can never truly escape from.

I know Sharma Ji, especially for someone who has spent his life here.

Aarav, this place has given me everything. I was able to fulfill all my family responsibilities because of it.

But why did you want to meet me?

I've heard about you in the news; you've become quite the figure!

What figure? It's just hype, nothing more.

I'm here because I have a job for you.

A job for me? Seriously, Aarav?

Yes, Sharma Ji, I want you to be my consultant and personal advisor.

Do you really think I'm capable of being your advisor? I'm just an ordinary stockbroker, and with technology advancing, people like us aren't really needed anymore.

Experience, Sharma Ji. You have tons of it, and that's valuable. I know you can give me the right advice because I see you as a father figure.

You know, I always told Param to give Aarav to me—I always wanted a son like you.

I've done everything for my family. I educated my only daughter well and made sure her marriage was proper. But I always felt your aunty made many sacrifices for me to achieve all this. My last wish is to take her on a world tour.

That's a fantastic idea, Sharma Ji! That's actually why I'm here. Take this job, and once we establish AVCL, you can take a long leave for your world tour. You're still young—only 56—you've got plenty of life left!

I don't see a reason to decline your offer, Aarav. Welcome to AVCL, Sharma Ji!

Thank you! I read in the newspaper that you started an AMC company, AVCL. What have you accomplished in the month since its launch?

I've secured all the licenses and regulatory clearances. I also set up an office with a finance and tech team working on projects I assigned.

So, you've been preparing early!

Yes, Sharma Ji, I've been planning this for the past year.

What about money? In an AMC, we usually attract clients and hedge their funds.

You're right, Sharma Ji, but money isn't a problem. I've invested my own funds, and I'm backed by Neil, so I have almost 1,000 crores on the table.

So you have enough funds, Aarav. However, we can't enter the market with just these funds, as it will limit our options.

Exactly, Sharma Ji! That's why I haven't entered the market directly.

We need a user base, Aarav.

I know Sharma Ji, but we don't have time to go the traditional route of acquiring clients.

Okay, if that's the case, we can acquire a firm that already has a user base. But we'd need funds well beyond 1,000 crores since we have to target a firm with at least half a million to a million retail clients to really make an impact in the stock market.

Aarav Ji, the magic in business lies in not revealing how it's done. We only believe what we can see, and it's the same with the market.

That's why I like you, Sharma Ji. You understand the market like no one else.

Regarding funds for acquisitions, I've mentioned my financial backing because you're my advisor. But outside of AVCL, it's known that I'm backed by Neil Ahuja, the CEO of Privisha Group, and people know my name too, so they'll trust that I have enough to offer.

But I'm not looking to acquire a firm outright. Instead, I want to enter into strategic partnerships where we get access to their customers in exchange for offering them stakes in our firm. Their firm would then act as an arm for customer relations while we handle all the business operations.

Aarav Ji, you've become quite sharp. This can indeed work.

Sharma Ji, you've been studying companies for years—can you suggest any that fit our requirements?

Solkar Finance Group. That's the company we should target. They have a platform for investing with a user base of 1 million, while their competitors have 10 million and above. Their retail platform is called SOLTRADE.

They operate in a traditional style, which is why they have such a small user base. They've also been looking to upgrade for a long time. They actually lack a creative CEO who can push for a greater market share.

Still, Sharma Ji, with only 1 million users, don't you think it will be difficult to convince them for a partnership?

Aarav Ji, if you can't convince, you shouldn't enter the stock market business at all. From what I see, you have a firm with advanced technology and the ability to generate ideas for improving business. We'll use this unique selling proposition (USP) to convince them, and I know they'll agree based on their current market position.

Great, Sharma Ji! You've done your research on SOLTRADE!

Aarav, this is my profession as a stockbroker. I must keep an eye on every company in the space.

Okay, then I'll ask Priyansha to schedule an appointment with SOLTRADE's owner.

Who's Priyansha?

She's my office coordinator.

I see.

So, tomorrow, first thing, we meet with SOLTRADE and make sure we seal the deal.

We will, Aarav. See you tomorrow!

Morning!

Sharma Ji, ready to roll?

We're all set! Just watch how I pull this off today.

Okay, Aarav, if you impress me, tea is on me at the tapri.

Deal, Sharma Ji! For tapri tea, I'd climb any mountain!

Sir, Mr. Solkar is ready to meet you.

Good Morning, Mr. Solkar! I'm Aarav, and this is my advisor, Sharma Ji.

Good morning, Aarav! Surprised to see you with an older advisor. That's rare these days, especially with so many young people around.

Mr. Solkar, I value experience above all else. Experience saves time, and I'm a bit tight on that, so it's gold for me.

You've earned a brownie point from me, Aarav. I believe in the power of experience.

Now, what's your proposal? I've already been briefed by my secretary about your agenda for a strategic partnership.

Mr. Solkar, I'm a straightforward guy. I've started an AMC firm called AVCL, and I want to partner with you to kickstart my business.

What's in it for me, Mr. Aarav?

Great question! You'll get a partner who will not only revamp your SOLTRADE platform but also scale your business to unimaginable heights.

Aarav, I can hire a firm to redesign my platform and suggest new business ideas. So that alone isn't enough to pique my interest.

First off, Mr. Solkar, you're speaking to someone who has redefined a business in under a year and scaled it up significantly. But if you need more, my AVCL has the funds to support your firm for a considerable time since it's backed by the CEO of the Privisha Group.

You know better than I do, Mr. Solkar, that redefining your product requires funds to stabilize it in the market, and no firm you hire will provide that for you.

I understand your point, Aarav, but building a user base is no small feat. I need more than just funds.

Alright, Mr. Solkar, what do you need exactly?

I need a 25% stake in your AVCL.

Mr. Solkar, 25% stakes in AVCL would be worth far more than your firm's current valuation.

Don't talk nonsense, Aarav. AVCL is practically worthless today, and it'll take time to reach a level where 25% stakes would be equal to my firm's valuation.

Aarav, 25% is too much for a new firm like AVCL. We might need to dilute shares for future funding from investors. Once you give away 25%, you'll struggle to dilute further. Plus, if you aim for an IPO, you might lose control of your own firm.

I know Sharma Ji, but I'm running out of options. So, Mr. Solkar, I'll offer you a final proposal: 21% stakes in AVCL.

I can't be too harsh on you, since you're here to help me grow my business. It's a deal. You'll give me 21% stakes in AVCL, and in return, you'll gain access to my company's resources, including my user base. You can also take operational control of the SOLTRADE platform, while I handle customer relationships.

Great, Mr. Solkar! You got everything you wanted. Without too much effort, you secured 21% stakes in a company backed by the Privisha Group and a strategic partnership to grow your business. It's a win-win deal for you!

Don't think I'm a fool; I understand perfectly. Granting you access to my 1 million customers means you could execute trades with little accountability. No amount of money can give you a state of business with no accountability. You've hit the jackpot with this deal, and I'm not left with many options, which is why I'm agreeing to this partnership.

I'm impressed, Mr. Solkar. You certainly understand this business well. Trust me, you can pitch to your customers that they can expect a 20% annual aggregate gain from the SOLTRADE platform—far better than what others offer.

I'll develop a whole new product within a month. We'll launch it together, allowing you to enter the retail trading market as well.

With a 50-50 partnership on the product.

Now we're talking like partners, Aarav! This proposal is accepted without objections.

Okay, Mr. Solkar, let's keep this under wraps. The day we launch our retail trading platform is when we'll announce our partnership.

Done, Aarav! I'll prepare the paperwork for signatures.

Yes, please, Mr. Solkar. I'll send my team heads to assist with customer access and operations. After this partnership, we'll essentially be one entity.

Indeed, Mr. Solkar, we will be.

I'll take your leave now, Mr. Solkar.

Okay, Aarav. I look forward to working together.

Sure, Mr. Solkar. Have a great day!

Sharma Ji, it's time for my tapri tea—I've won our bet!

Absolutely, Aarav! The moment we reach the office, we're heading to that tea stall across the road from your building.

Looking forward to it, Sharma Ji!

Shyam, two cups of tea, please.

Here's our tea. Aarav, one thing is clear: Mr. Solkar is a savvy businessman. He knew we were after his resources, especially his customer base.

But honestly, I think we played our cards right and saved nearly 9% on that deal. It could have easily been 29-30%.

You deserve a lot of credit for that! You really caught on to what I was hinting at.

Aarav Ji, at my age, understanding like that is more a feature than a skill.

We need to ramp things up and get our team moving; I want to launch that platform in less than a month.

Absolutely! Timing is everything in the stock market.

Tomorrow, I'll show you how our HFA is designed, specifically for the stock market.

I've heard a lot about HFA. I used to work at a finance firm that used it, but I found it tough to handle, especially when the market gets wild.

Exactly, HFA is like a nuclear warhead. If you launch it without understanding, it'll be a disaster. And it requires substantial funds to execute in zones for meaningful gains.

HFA typically captures small changes that humans often miss when trading.

But you wouldn't use a nuclear warhead to swat mosquitoes!

When used correctly, HFAs can act like a nuclear reactor, providing stable, clean energy regularly, thus creating reliable funds.

So, let's start with a design review tomorrow. We're on a tight schedule; everyone needs to be ready for a launch within a month. Once we roll out this platform, we'll begin executing those HFAs.

Okay, Aarav, I'll handle all the formalities for this partnership and see you tomorrow for the demo.

Roger that, Sharma Ji.

Hi Aarav, is that you, Shivanya? Am I dreaming?

Yes, it's me, Mr. AVCL. What brings you here? You don't want me here?

Ms. Sen, if it were up to me, I'd keep you in my sight all the time.

And what would you do then?

I'd admire you like someone appreciates a mountain's beauty.

Why, Aarav? Why are you like this?

Not with everyone, Shivanya. I'm usually pretty serious, but when I see you, a different side of me comes out.

That's clear to everyone.

But seriously, how did you end up here?

I was passing by, saw the AVCL hoarding, and remembered it's your new firm. I decided to check it out from my car and then spotted you having tea.

So, you're saying you're keeping tabs on me? You just had to visit me at a roadside tea stall?

Aarav, I'm human too! I can't explain why I'm curious about you or why I wanted to see you.

Listen, I may have been rude before, but I've spent time abroad, so I'm straightforward and honest. What I feel, I say. I honestly don't know why I'm here, so don't ask me. There's something between us, but I can't put my finger on it.

Shivanya, you always ask why I act this way with you. It's because I see purity in you, which is rare. You love deeply, and you have standards, hence the rudeness. Honestly, your rudeness is my favorite part of you.

Why are you drinking tea from here? Don't they serve in your office?

Shivanya, this isn't ordinary tea. Once I drink it, my mind kicks into overdrive and does the impossible.

You're joking, right? That can't be true!

If that were the case, everyone would be drinking from roadside stalls.

Statistically speaking, they actually are! Roadside tea consumption is much higher than anywhere else.

If that's true, I'll have to try it! Are you sure, Shivanya? Tomorrow's headlines will read: "Shivanya Sen Spotted at a Roadside Tea Stall." How will you handle that?

Aarav, shut up! Alright, I'll get one for you.

Shyam Ji, make your best tea and serve it in a kulhad for madam.

Here you go, Shivanya.

I know the name, but I can't quite recall it right now.

It's called kulhad, and it makes this tea taste heavenly!

It's good, Aarav! Actually, it tastes very different from what I'm used to. How much for this?

Don't worry, Shivanya; I'll take care of it.

Aarav, I don't let anyone pay my bills!

Okay, Shivanya, here's the payment for the two cups.

Wait, you gave him 2000 rupees for two cups of tea? Is that too little? Should I pay more?

Actually, Aarav, I only have 2000 in cash right now.

Shivanya, since you paid, that's fine. It's more than enough for tea served to "The Shivanya Sen."

So, how's Lakshya doing?

He's great, busy expanding into the internet sector. You must've heard about our upcoming internet arm.

Sounds like he's a busy man! Yes, very busy.

And what about you, Mr. Aarav? What's the plan with AVCL?

Nothing much; I just thought it'd be good to start something of my own, so I launched AVCL, an AMC firm.

That's a bold move! Most would stay at The Privisha Group and capitalize on personal gain.

Yes, you're right, Shivanya. But I tend to do things differently. Sometimes, people get stuck chasing small gains for too long. If you have a good idea, you should pursue it, even if it means pushing your boundaries.

I can't believe you were a waiter once, Aarav! You're like a completely different person now, talking about pushing comfort zone boundaries.

That's the magic of life and knowledge, Shivanya.

Honestly, I'm more curious about what you're doing than my own business!

Please, if you keep praising me like that, I won't be able to sleep tonight! And about your business—you're not doing much there, are you?

Aarav, I want to contribute fully, but my father doesn't really want me involved. He only allows my brother to take part.

Why's that, Shivanya?

He thinks my mother passed away due to her being too wrapped up in work and not taking enough time for herself. He doesn't want to see that happen to me.

I know it sounds strange, considering he's such a big industrialist, but he's also just a father who loves his children. Any parent would feel that way.

I get it, Shivanya. He's close to you and likely worries that if you're too busy with work, he'll be lonely, especially at his age.

Aarav, I have to go; I'm running late.

Shivanyaaaaa.

What, Aarav?

Stay just a little longer!

No, I really have to go. Why are you acting like I'm your girlfriend? If you keep insisting, I might consider staying.

I'm not your girlfriend! Get that through your head. I only believe in marriage. Nothing else.

So, you mean I'll marry you? You're clearly in your own fictional world. I'm getting engaged to Lakshya in less than a year.

I know, Shivanya; you've mentioned it before. But until you're engaged, I can still make my moves!

What moves are you talking about? None of it will work—don't waste your time; focus on your AVCL. Your chances are zero, so just stop.

Ms. Shivanya, when was the last time you stopped to check out someone's office or had tea with someone at a roadside stall?

Think about it, Shivanya. You might realize what my chances really are.

Aarav, bye! Take care.

Thanks, love.

Aarav, I will kill you!

Don't do that; I'll be your future husband!

Aarav, you're disgusting!

Listen, Shivanya, take care of yourself. I'm heading out now but will see you later.

Thanks! I want you to see me forever.

Aaraaaaaav!!!!

Bye, Shivanya.

Shivanya leaves.

Rishi, let's kick off your presentation. Sharma Ji, feel free to ask any questions about HFA and the new platform.

Sure, Aarav! We've developed a High-Frequency Algorithm (HFA) for two main purposes: first, to identify stocks whose behavior deviates from their traditional patterns over the past 1, 3, and 6 months. If a stock remains stable for too long and then experiences fluctuations beyond 7-10% of its price, we label it a "hot stock" that could erupt like a volcano.

We have a team of analysts monitoring these hot stocks to understand the reasons behind these changes. If we determine that the fluctuations suggest something significant, we'll decide to trade.

To facilitate trading, we've developed an algorithm for High-Frequency Trading (HFT). For a target stock, we'll use investor accounts to place trades simultaneously with these algorithms. The execution time for these trades is very quick, allowing us to capture movements and significantly profit from them.

Two key points: we won't ride the whole bullish or bearish candle. Instead, we'll trade between the high and low of a candle based on whether the trade is bullish or bearish.

What's the process for starting an algorithm to execute an HFT?

Good question, Sharma Ji. Once we finalize trading in these hot stocks, our analysts will perform level analyses. This will give us two executing levels for HFT: PLOE (Price Level of Execution) and PLOT (Price Level of Termination). Since all algorithms are model-based, these levels are generated from equations created by our data scientists after analyzing the market to meet our needs.

And, of course, there will be stop-loss measures in place. The key thing about HFT is that once executed, it can't be terminated, so we need to be careful before starting. Given the tight levels on charts, there's not much time to make adjustments.

But shouldn't there be a timeout feature to terminate the HFT if the expected action doesn't happen?

Exactly! For instance, if we predict a bullish trade that should rise from 100 to 120 in one candle, but we don't see that jump within half the candle's duration, the HFT should automatically square off our position.

Is that feature available?

Yes, it is, but the execution timeline is just over half the duration of a candle.

Who suggested that, Rishi?

I did, Sharma Ji. Often, people prematurely square off their trades early in a candle's duration. When they exit, they see the candle reach their predicted level. This behavior is pretty common among intraday traders, so I want us to be patient with our approach.

Correct, Aarav. Patience is key in the stock market. To excel, you need patience and analytical risk-taking skills.

Indeed, Sharma Ji, it truly is.

Let's move forward. We've covered the HFA model for executing HFTs, and now I'll showcase our new SOLTrade platform, which provides customers with access to both cryptocurrency and stock trading.

The app will feature two distinct models for stocks and cryptocurrencies. What's crucial about this app is its near-zero lag in the trading process, enabling day traders to execute their trades accurately. For cryptocurrencies, we've developed a robust platform supporting every major currency. This will be the only platform in the country that allows users to manage both portfolios with minimal hassle.

Given the heavy regulations surrounding cryptocurrency trading, we've designed this module in collaboration with government officials to ensure that all transactions are legal and trustworthy. Users won't have to worry about transactions—any regulatory deductions will be automatically handled before transferring gains to their personal accounts.

Aarav, this platform is a game changer because of the scale our team has achieved.

Yes, Sharma Ji, the goal is to provide users with access to every form of trading on a single platform, allowing seamless transactions. With government involvement, the fear of illegality surrounding cryptocurrencies will be mitigated. Our analysts have done an excellent job of reducing trading lag to almost zero.

So, if I understand correctly, we'll earn from HFTs for AVCL, and SOLTrade will provide us with our share of the profits, allowing us to consolidate funds quickly?

Generally, Sharma Ji, I prefer not to chase quick money, but sometimes there's no time to waste. So yes, I'm targeting six months to build enough wealth.

Enough wealth for what, Aarav? You've got something else in mind, don't you?

Sharma Ji, to achieve the greatest success, you need to pull the longest strings in this complex web of connections.

I'm not following you, Aarav.

You'll understand when the time is right, but for now, the success of AVCL is our only focus.

Rishi, make sure we conduct an extensive three-week test run to identify any glitches in the platform and especially with HFA. After that, we'll go live in the fourth week.

Got it, Aarav.

Sharma Ji, what launch date do you suggest?

I believe March 28th would be ideal.

If you say so, Sharma Ji, March 28th will be the launch day for SOLTRADE 2.0. Please inform Mr. Solkar and take care of the formalities.

Aarav, we also need to be aware that launching on March 28th coincides with the financial year-end, which may lead to significant market corrections.

Absolutely, Sharma Ji; that's an important consideration.

Alright, everyone, let's get to work. Rishi will handle the app, HFA, and Sharma Ji will take care of the partnership formalities.

Day - March 28th

SOLTRADE 2.0 is set to create an ecosystem where users can manage their entire portfolio on one platform, allowing for seamless trading. The speed of execution with SOLTRADE 2.0 is incredibly fast, making it ideal for day traders.

With the launch of SOLTRADE 2.0, we're proud to announce our partnership with AVCL. SOLTRADE 2.0 will be fully operated by AVCL, while the customer side will be managed by the Solkar Group. In this partnership, the Solkar Group will acquire a 21% stake in AVCL.

I'd like to invite Mr. Aarav, CEO of AVCL, to share his thoughts on this partnership.

Thank you, Mr. Solkar. I know everyone is curious why I transitioned from The Privisha Group to launching the AVCL and Solkar Group partnership. In today's fast-paced world, we need to adapt quickly.

As for SOLTRADE 2.0, it will offer customers a single platform for both stock and cryptocurrency trading. In this day and age, people need everything in one place to avoid the hassle of juggling multiple platforms.

I want to congratulate the entire teams at AVCL and Solkar Group for their outstanding work in launching SOLTRADE 2.0 in record time. Rishi, our CTO, has been instrumental in this development. Kudos to you, Rishi!

Now, I'm open to questions from the media.

Mr. Aarav, doesn't giving all your resources and 21% of AVCL to the Solkar Group seem counterintuitive? Can you explain what the benefits are for AVCL?

Great question. By partnering with SOLTRADE 2.0, we're securing a 50-50 share in the financial business. The 21% stake allows us to tap into the Solkar Group's user base, which will provide us a head start in a competitive market. We have a solid tech environment, and Solkar Group's reputation for customer service makes this partnership beneficial for both sides, allowing us to offer an exceptional product.

Mr. Aarav, can you elaborate on your transition from the service industry to fintech?

Well, I have a finance background, so it's not as polarizing a shift as it seems. Technology is the future, and everything will revolve around it, so understanding technology is essential—it's a natural progression.

We've officially launched SOLTRADE 2.0 successfully, Sharma Ji!

Yes, Aarav, it's a fantastic start! Let's celebrate with tea at our favorite spot.

You know, Sharma Ji, I'm not a fan of parties; I prefer living life simply.

I know you have an old-school approach to living.

Now, we must keep our eyes wide open regarding these HFAs; they're crucial to our revenue.

Exactly, Sharma Ji. While revenue from SOLTRADE 2.0 will recoup our investments, profits from HFTs will be our real earnings.

FIVE MONTHS LATER……

In just five months, SOLTRADE 2.0 has doubled its customer base and significantly increased revenue. Meanwhile, AVCL's revenue has skyrocketed, nearing an impressive $1 billion within six months. Let's delve deeper into this story.

Generating close to $1 billion is monumental, Aarav. Not only is SOLTRADE 2.0 contributing to this revenue, but our HFAs are also raking in substantial profits. Achieving this level of business in just six months is nothing short of a record.

Sharma Ji, when you combine technology with experience, you create unimaginable wealth. The key is to believe in the process.

Our sponsorships and partnerships with leading players in cloud computing and cutting-edge technology, like AI, have established AVCL as a formidable force in the market.

Sharma Ji, you can definitely plan that world tour with Aunty now!

I plan to, Aarav. But you might be surprised to know that your aunt wants me to take on the COO role at AVCL with full dedication. She's enjoying the praise I'm receiving due to AVCL's success.

She always dreamed of seeing me succeed at this level.

That's fantastic, Sharma Ji! You absolutely deserve it.

Aarav? What is it, Rishi?

I need you both in the operations center right away.

Sharma Ji, I think Rishi has spotted something significant in the market.

Tell us, Rishi, what's the urgent news?

The stock of the government's chip-based public entity has plummeted by nearly 25% in just two days. This drop is due to rising tensions and supply chain issues in the countries supplying raw materials.

If we bet on this collapse, it could be our most profitable trade yet. It seems likely that this stock will remain bearish for some time. We can leverage our HFA during this decline to maximize profits.

Aarav, Rishi is onto something; it looks like a complete downward spiral for this stock. We can seriously benefit from this.

It's the perfect opportunity for AVCL to surpass that $1 billion mark by a significant margin.

Rishi, what's the status of all companies related to silicon chips globally?

U.S. and European companies are bullish, showing gains of about 20%, while Southeast Asian companies are feeling the impact of the crisis.

There's not just a scarcity of raw materials; we're also facing a trade war with Asian countries, particularly concerning silicon chips.

Recently, products from Asian countries based on silicon chips have made significant strides, leading many Western companies to go out of business.

Got it, Rishi. We won't let this downward trend continue.

What do you mean, Aarav?

I suggest we buy significant shares of this firm to halt its decline.

Have you lost your mind, Aarav? This is like walking into the ocean while a tsunami is approaching!

What are you thinking, Aarav?

Sharma Ji, trust me. It's a government firm; buying this stock could be the key to our company's future.

I believe we have enough funds for this move, but let's ensure we place a long position using our HFA.

I'm not sure I understand, Aarav.

I know, Rishi, just do it and have faith in me. I promise you won't regret this.

Mr. Aarav has been honored with the CEO of the Year award by Financial Times! His company, AVCL, has made waves in the finance sector, thanks to strategic partnerships with SOLKAR Group and key alliances in cloud computing and AI, giving AVCL a significant boost.

Aarav's achievement is particularly noteworthy as Emilink's renowned CEO, Lakshya Seth, has held this title for the past three years and was a strong contender again this year.

Experts at Financial Times have highlighted the staggering scale of AVCL's business and praised Aarav for his extraordinary efforts in positioning AVCL through vital partnerships.

That's all for now from GlobeNews Prime. Stay tuned for more updates!

Shivanya? What's up, Maya? Why are you calling so early?

It's 11 o'clock! Wake up!

I'm feeling a bit lazy today, Maya.

You should go see Lakshya.

Maya, I just met him two days ago. He's swamped with the launch of Emilink's optical fiber internet service.

Did you hear?

What, Maya?

Who won the CEO of the Year award from Financial Times this year?

Lakshya won it again for the fourth time.

Oh! That's why you called! I'm going to meet him today and congratulate him.

Actually, it's not Lakshya who won.

What?

Yeah, it's true.

Then who won it, Maya?

Surprisingly, Aarav from AVCL is the winner!

You're joking, right? This can't be!

Shivanya, check for yourself; it's true!

Oh my god! Aarav actually won! This is insane—$1 billion in six months? This guy is incredible!

I know, right? He's completely off the charts! But I see a lot changing, especially concerning you.

What changes are you talking about, Maya?

Don't deny it, Shivanya. I haven't seen that spark in your eyes regarding Lakshya for the past six months.

You two are supposed to get engaged soon, but I don't see any real connection between you.

But you mention your meeting with Aarav almost every time we talk.

I can see the excitement on your face when Aarav's name comes up.

Whenever AVCL achieves something—like launching SOLTRADE 2.0 or forming strategic partnerships—I notice you keeping a close watch on him. I've even seen you following his podcasts and interviews.

Maya, it's nothing; I'm just curious about what he's up to. I'm in finance, so what happens in that world is my thing.

You're denying it again.

Maya, there's nothing between us. We've hardly met.

Who said you have to meet every day for something to develop? You're overthinking it, Maya.

Shivanya, meet Lakshya today. He might be a bit upset about the award.

Not really; he's won it three times before and is busy with the expansion. I'll call to check on him but will see him this weekend.

Alright, Shivanya. But please, don't complicate things. I'm warning you: stay away from Aarav.

Okay, Maya, I understand, but I'm not interested in Aarav. We have a little history, so we meet occasionally—that's all.

Good, Shivanya. Now wake up and go to work.

Okay, Maya, bye!

Shivanya checks her phone for notifications.

Who's messaging me now?

Don't you think you should congratulate me?

Aarav? What makes you think that?

That's called manners.

Oh, I see—manners! What about not picking up my call?

Shivanya, I left my phone in the car that day; it was my fault, I'm sorry. But I called you afterward, and you didn't pick up.

Do one thing: why don't you throw that phone away? It's useless, Mr. CEO of the Year! By the way, courtesy suggests you could have tried another way to reach me or at least come to see me.

After that last meeting, when you told me, "I'm not your girlfriend," how am I supposed to think of doing that?

So, do you only show manners to your girlfriend? What about acquaintances?

My bad, Shivanya. I'm not as well-mannered as you are. But I'd love it if you could grace this poor guy with your beautiful face!

Oh, I see! Mr. CEO. Don't get carried away; I'm not coming to see you even in your dreams!

Conversation ends.

Love is Cooking?

I'm so unlucky, I swear! I can feel you laughing at me up there.

Sir, yes, Shyam ji? Your tea is ready, and who are you talking to? There's no one around.

Nothing, Shyam ji. I just have a habit of chatting with God.

What, sir?

Never mind, Shyam ji. You carry on.

Can I ask why you think you're so unlucky?

Shivanya arrives.

Shivanyaaaa! What a surprise! You came to see me!

Don't get too excited. I'm here to congratulate you on your win, unlike you, I have manners.

You know, I had a feeling you'd show up. Care for some kulhad tea?

Aarav, it's easy to predict where to find you at this time of day.

Unlike you, Shivanya, I'm not a celebrity, so tracking me is pretty simple. I love this tea spot—I come here multiple times a day!

Here's your tea. You know, I don't understand why I end up doing things I normally wouldn't, all because of you.

I know, Shivanya. We share a strong connection.

How do you know that, Aarav?

Because I can feel it. Maya warned me not to meet you, but here I am anyway.

That's exactly what I was saying about our connection.

I must admit, I'm impressed by your business acumen. You're sharp and have a clear vision.

Thank you! Your story is quite compelling.

Don't say that, Shivanya. Think about Lakshya for a moment.

What about him?

He might be upset to hear you praising me.

Why? You deserve the praise, and I always give credit where it's due.

That's why you set such high standards, Ms. Shivanya Sen. I absolutely love it!

What did you say, Aarav?

I was talking about your standards—nothing else. Better?

So, what about your upcoming engagement? I guess it's only a few months away?

What about it, Aarav?

Everything is on track. We've already contracted an event management company for the arrangements.

Shivanya, I'm not talking about the arrangements.

Then what are you saying, Mr. CEO?

Tell me, why did you come to see me? If you're so certain about your engagement, you should be with him, especially knowing he might be frustrated to see me win.

Aarav, Lakshya is very intelligent; he doesn't get upset over trivial things. He's also busy with his new venture.

No, Shivanya, that's a lie. You came here because you wanted to see me. It's been a while since we met, and you miss me just as I miss you every day.

Aarav, you must be joking! I'm missing you?

I'm not kidding, Shivanya.

What do you mean?

I mean, Ms. Shivanya Sen, that you like me and want me around. But because you're The Shivanya Sen, you can't convince yourself that you like Aarav, who was just a waiter when we first met.

Don't talk to me like that, Aarav.

Shivanya, I respect you. But if I don't bring reality to light today, it could get serious, and you won't admit it until it's too late. I can't let that happen.

Aarav, I came here because I see you as a friend, and I believe you understand me.

I understand you, Shivanya, because we have that connection. But sorry, we aren't friends. I would love to be close to you, but I think it's time for us to part ways.

What are you talking about, Aarav? I don't understand.

Shivanya, you're getting engaged soon, and I know you'll never admit you like me. It's fair to say we should part ways because I know where this leads.

Why are you suddenly talking about parting, Aarav? You wanted me to come and meet you!

I know, Shivanya. But I also realize that whatever we have will only complicate your life. Your friend Maya is right; you shouldn't see me. You should be with Lakshya now.

I don't understand why you're acting so strangely, Aarav. I know I'm getting engaged, but I also know how I feel about you. I see you as a friend, that's it.

Great, Shivanya! Since you're so clear about everything, I'm telling you I don't want to be your friend anymore. We shouldn't meet, talk, or message.

Fine then, Mr. Aarav. Maya was right; I've given you unnecessary attention, and you'll never truly fit into our society. You might have money, but class isn't bought. You'll always be seen as a waiter.

It was my mistake to think we could be friends. I forgot that a waiter and a Shivanya Sen can't be friends.

Get lost, Mr. Aarav.

Shivanya storms out.

Did I just hear your heart break, Mr. Aarav?

Sri says: I knew she'd break your heart one day, and your respect too, but you never listened to me.

Sri, I'd rather have my heart broken than see her leave.

What do you mean, Aarav?

Sri, she loves me, but her mind won't let her accept it. She's always so sure of what she wants, how her life should be, and then I come along—someone she never pictured herself with.

So, you see how hard it is for her to accept her feelings for me.

The problem is that she's so driven that she'll marry Lakshya and later realize her feelings for me. I can't let her make that mistake. It's better for us to stay apart.

Aarav, Shivanya is an adult. Don't tell me she doesn't realize she loves you.

Sri, she's confused. She's been raised like a princess, accustomed to a different lifestyle. You wouldn't understand.

I'm not interested in how your dream girl was raised or why she's confused about her feelings. But I'm glad you're choosing to part ways with her.

I'm seriously so unlucky. Anyway, why are you here, Sri?

To celebrate your win, Aarav. I'm so proud of you! From waiter to CEO of the Year—you've done the unimaginable!

Thanks, Sri. Yes, there's a party planned by Rishi. You all enjoy.

You're not coming, Aarav?

You know, Sri, I don't like parties.

Shivanya? What's up? Why did you call me over urgently?

Maya, you were right about Aarav—he thinks way too highly of himself! Who is he to tell me I can't understand my own feelings? Who gave him the right to decide we should part ways? I was just trying to be polite and congratulate him. And now he thinks I'm in love with him!

Maya, these low-class people may earn money, but their mindset is just pathetic. How can he even think I have feelings for him? Why is he acting all noble?

Relax, Shivanya. So, you two won't meet anymore?

Forget meeting him—I won't ever lay eyes on him again!

One Month Later…

Where's Aarav?

Sharma Ji: He went to a meeting with some partners. When will he be back?

Anytime now, Sharma Ji. But why do you want to see him?

Nothing, I just want to talk.

Oh, Sharma Ji, you're here! I was just about to call you. Aarav, you've arrived!

Yes, Sharma Ji. Who's with you?

This is Mayur Tyagi.

Okay, Sharma Ji, give me the details. Why is he here? Let's talk in my cabin.

Aarav, Mayur is the son of my dear friend. He started a company focused on building rockets to launch satellites for various purposes, like sensing and environmental monitoring. He had a team of scientists from reputable institutes, but they faced some initial failures in testing their rocket engines, which forced Mayur to seek more funds to keep development on track. He now only holds 25% of his own startup and has lost the power to make decisions.

He's fine with that; he just wants the company to help people. But now, the majority stakeholders want to shift the company's focus from rockets to building complex satellites to sell to small countries and agencies. He's come to me for help because he thinks I can assist as COO of AVCL.

Got it, Sharma Ji. Mayur, can you launch these rockets in a month?

Yes, Aarav. My team has done all the necessary tests, and the structure is ready. The stakeholders are just worried that if we launch and it fails, they'll lose their investments.

Can you deploy your team to build satellites to provide internet services?

Yes, that's not too difficult.

The tricky part, Mayur, is that the satellites need to be deployed in a way that eliminates the traditional lag associated with satellite-based internet. I want these satellites to deliver fast internet with almost no lag.

We can deploy a constellation of satellites in very low Earth orbits to minimize distance and improve connectivity. We'll also use advanced communication devices to enhance transmitters and receivers for quick signal reception, ensuring smooth internet functionality.

If you promise to launch these satellites within a month, then we have a deal. I'll help you regain control of your company by giving you 48% and making you CEO with operational decision-making authority. I'll manage the business with 51%.

I can promise you that, Aarav, but how will you reclaim the company from the investors?

Don't worry, Mayur. I'll leverage fear and greed to my advantage.

Get to work, and you'll have your company back in a week. Rishi will send you all the project details. We'll rename your company "SATSKY" and launch a product called "SATNET," an internet service provider that connects even the most remote areas to high-speed internet.

SATSKY sounds cool, and SATNET is a brilliant idea!

Absolutely, Mayur. Let's get moving!

Shivanya, why aren't you eating?

Lakshya: I just don't feel like it.

What's wrong, Shivanya?

Nothing, Lakshya.

I can see you're not interested in anything lately. Something's bothering you, and I want to know what it is.

Lakshya, I told you, I'm just a bit burned out. I'm planning to take a break for a few weeks to focus on my hobbies.

Good idea! Take some time off and explore your interests. If you want, we could go somewhere, like the mountains or the beach.

No need for that, Lakshya. I know you're busy with your expansion plans.

Alright, as you wish.

Excuse me, sir, this is your complimentary dessert.

Complimentary dessert? For what?

Sir, Ambrosia is celebrating Aarav's achievements in business since he started as a waiter in this restaurant.

Oh! So, Mr. Aarav is being celebrated here.

And for you as well.

Thanks, but I won't have it. I'm not feeling well.

Excuse me, I'll have it—just serve it to me.

Shivanya, I thought you weren't eating today.

Yes, Lakshya, but this is dessert, and you know how much I love Ambrosia's desserts!

Go ahead and enjoy it then; it's complimentary.

Lakshya, you know about Aarav?

Yes, Shivanya, I know. I also know about the incident where you shouted at him at the party. But that was justified since it was his mistake.

So, have you ever met him?

No, Lakshya. Why would I meet him? I don't know him, and there's no reason for us to talk, let alone meet.

Shivanya, I have to say, his journey is nothing short of a miracle. I don't know how he made it so far. Sometimes I wonder if he's genuinely talented or if there's something else at play.

Lakshya, you can't succeed on that scale without talent. He must have it.

I don't know, Shivanya. I've seen many like him who rise quickly only to vanish without a trace.

People like Aarav often achieve rapid success, but without a future vision, they end up failing. Once they get access to large sums of money, it's hard for them to resist a lavish lifestyle, especially if they've faced scarcity before.

Lakshya, I don't think Aarav is the type to get caught up in a luxurious lifestyle. From where I stand, he's brilliant. Just having the courage to leave his COO position at Privisha Group to start AVCL is impressive!

That kind of courage is only found in those who have deep insights into the future and a clear vision of their place in it.

We'll see, Shivanya, in time, what he makes of himself.

I'm done with my food. Let me drop you off.

Okay, Lakshya, let's go.

We've arrived at your place, Shivanya.

Thanks, Lakshya. Bye!

Shivanya. Lakshya stopped her by holding her hand.

What are you doing, Lakshya?

Shivanya, we're getting engaged in two months, but we haven't had much quality time together. I love you, and I've tried to tell you this many times, but I couldn't find the right moment. I want you to know I'll do whatever it takes to make you happy. I'll take care of you for life. You mean everything to me—like a blessing from above. I'm lucky to have you, and I feel like I deserve you. We both have high standards in life, and we complement each other perfectly. I'm sure we'll make a great couple.

Lakshya, I don't know how to respond. You know my father thinks you're a good choice for me, and that's why I agreed. I've always trusted his advice because I know it's for my best.

But I'm not sure about my feelings right now. I need time to process this. I don't want you to feel bad, but I need to get into the right mindset for this relationship.

Take your time, Shivanya. I understand it's all happening a bit fast for you. I just wanted you to know how I feel.

Thanks for understanding, Lakshya. Bye.

Bye, Shivanya.

The Next Morning at the AVCL Office

If I want to enter the internet service business, I need to create some space for it.

What do you mean, Aarav? What space?

Sharma Ji: Mayur will take almost a month to launch the satellites, and then another month will be needed to set up the service and complete all necessary steps after the satellites are in orbit. Only then can we announce SATNET services in the country. Until then, I need to ensure no major advancements happen in the internet service sector.

You're right, Aarav, but EMILINK has been targeting the internet service sector for a while now, and their expansion plans are in full swing. They want to replicate their success in telecom.

The upside is that optical fiber internet takes time to set up, but their speed is unbeatable. I know what they're up to, Sharma Ji.

But Aarav, before we think about creating space in the market, we should focus on getting regulatory approval for this project. It's a first-of-its-kind project, and the government won't approve it quickly.

Remember that silicon chip trade where we took significant losses to stop government interference?

Yes, Aarav.

Well, the government knows who holds their shares, even if we're taking heavy losses.

Oh, I see, Aarav. You're a genius. That trade was a strategic move to convince the government to approve SATNET faster.

I had SATNET in mind, Sharma Ji, but I knew it wouldn't happen soon. Still, whenever it does, I'll need government support. I saw an opportunity to help a government firm, and I took it, believing it would pay off in the future.

Aarav, your vision impresses me as a businessman.

Thanks, Sharma Ji. Business isn't just about profit; sometimes, you need to accept losses for larger future opportunities.

Also, Sharma Ji, we should offer a partnership to the government to support their scheme for internet access in every corner of the nation. SATNET is the fastest way to implement this scheme. I doubt they'll reject it.

It'll save them a lot of resources and money.

Indeed, Aarav. I'll handle all the approvals; don't worry about that.

Now, let's shift our focus back to creating space in the market.

Sharma Ji, what I'm about to show you is called the Iceberg Effect. Rishi advises you not to try this at home, as this stunt is under expert supervision.

Okay, Aarav, but what exactly will you do?

Tell me, Sharma Ji, what do you think of when you see an iceberg?

It looks small because only a tiny part is above water, but it's much stronger underneath and can destroy anything that hits it.

Exactly, Sharma Ji. Today, we'll create that small visible portion of the iceberg, and you'll see how the rest of it forms from people's fears.

Rishi, what analysis do we have on EMILINK shares?

Aarav, EMILINK shows a strong bullish trend, but it's consolidating at one level.

What's the timeframe for this consolidation, Rishi?

The consolidation phase has been visible for the last month.

That's great news. It means there's pressure building up, preparing for a breakout. But here's the trick: once a dip starts forming, the mindset shifts, and consolidation becomes a signal for a major sell-off.

We'll create that dip, just like the visible portion of an iceberg, and the signal from that dip will automatically form the rest of the iceberg. In fact, sharp traders will be looking for those dips to catch early signs of a sell-off.

When they start shorting the stock, those watching these sharp traders will follow suit, triggering a chain reaction that leads to a massive sell-off and chaos in the stock market.

Aarav, how can you be so sure these sharp traders will follow your lead?

Sharma Ji, what's your take on EMILINK shares?

Based on fundamental analysis, the company has a strong presence in the sector and leads the market. Plus, it's backed by the Sen group, so it's financially sound. My analysis: it's a must-buy.

Exactly, Sharma Ji. But these traders are called sharp because they don't follow general notions; they react to what they see. They're not long-term investors; they want short-term gains, and retail traders often ride their waves.

The point is, what they see will be true, so I'm confident this major sell-off will happen.

But how does this buy us time to establish our business, Aarav?

When this sell-off happens out of nowhere, it'll create a shock effect for EMILINK. All their focus will shift to figuring out how it happened and how to control it.

If the sell-off exceeds 10% over a few consecutive days, they could take a year to recover.

So, EMILINK will redirect all its resources to stabilize their existing telecom business to regain their previous status and will likely pause their fiber expansion plan.

Yes, Rishi. Get your HFA ready for implementation.

Aarav, one important suggestion: for this to work, the HFT should mimic human behavior. The accounts used by HFT should take a reasonable amount of time to execute trades, just like a human would.

That's right, Sharma Ji. That's why I value experience like gold. The HFT will handle around 100,000 accounts for executing trades, and their completion time will match an average human's.

EMILINK will definitely analyze this sell-off and suspect an individual behind it; it should appear as a human act.

Got it, Aarav. So your HFT setup for selling off EMILINK shares using 100,000 accounts is all set?

Since every account already has shares in their portfolio, we've got a legitimate start for this major sell-off.

Great, Rishi. Let's go. Sell it!

Sold, Aarav.

Now let's grab some tea and come back in a couple of hours to check the outcome.

Breaking News: A shocking turn of events in the stock market! The telecom leader EMILINK has seen its shares plummet by 12% in just three hours. Experts view this as a major sell-off, with some suggesting it's a significant correction. They blame the company for prematurely planning to expand into the internet service sector without solidifying their position in telecom.

If expert predictions hold true, EMILINK shares could face serious declines, with this 12% drop merely a warning sign. Stay tuned for more on StockN.

Lakshya, what's going on? Why are EMILINK shares tanking?

I'm heading to the office.

Shivanya, I can't believe this is happening.

Shivanya arrived at the office.

Everyone is in the control room, including you, Lakshya.

Okay, Shivanya. Now tell me, what really triggered this? I'm asking everyone; the floor is open.

Shivanya: Yes, Dhruv. I warned that entering the internet service sector could hurt us, especially since we're still new compared to EMILINK.

Did you raise this concern with Lakshya?

Yes, I did. I told Lakshya multiple times to take a bit more time for expansion.

Lakshya, what do you say?

Shivanya, you know there's never a perfect time for expansion. We've already secured a significant market share in telecom, and our speed is what has helped EMILINK grow rapidly. Speed is our USP—how can you expect us to slow down?

I understand, Lakshya, but the expansion decision isn't the reason for this sell-off. It's something else.

Can I say something, Shivanya?

Upadhyay Ji, I know it'll take time for you to process this. I understand that quick market changes are hard to grasp, especially at your age. If you need time to analyze, I'm sorry, but we don't have any.

Lakshya, let him speak.

Thank you, ma'am. I am very loyal to your father and respect him because he always valued experience, unlike this new generation, which thinks experience is outdated.

From my experience, I can tell this sell-off was created; it didn't just happen.

Could you elaborate, Upadhyay Ji?

I mean, ma'am, someone started this intentionally.

How is that possible?

I don't fully understand the methods, but this looks fabricated. News of a stock market sell-off spreads like wildfire, so it must have been initiated at an early stage, and then the market took over.

I can also tell you this was done by someone with deep pockets. Creating that initial dip requires significant funds. Their intentions are unclear, but they are targeting EMILINK.

Lakshya, what does our tech team say?

Shivanya, no HFT or computer-aided action was involved; the crash is purely a normal sell-off by regular investors.

Thank you, Upadhyay Ji. I also value experience like my father. From today onward, you will report to me. I believe you're correct. This seems like a fabricated action; a sudden 12% drop in EMILINK shares doesn't just happen.

I want you to use any resources necessary to find out how this was done.

Don't wait for approval; I'm the COO of this company, and you have my full support.

Ma'am, I'll provide a detailed report tomorrow.

I'll be waiting, Upadhyay Ji.

Shivanya, what's going on? You've suddenly taken charge.

Lakshya, stocks falling is common, but a drop without a clear reason is concerning.

I get it, Shivanya. I'm the CEO of this company, and I'll figure out how to stabilize our stocks.

Great! Let's divide our tasks. You handle resource allocation and strategy development to boost our stock, while I'll investigate who did this and their motives.

But Shivanya, the downside is that I'll have to pause our internet service expansion plan.

Lakshya, it'll take about a year for our stock to stabilize after this hit. If it's down by 12% today, retail traders will likely hit the lower circuit tomorrow.

One year isn't a significant delay for our internet services expansion. We can't risk losing our telecom business while trying to grow elsewhere.

So until EMILINK's stock stabilizes, we should hold off on expansion. Plus, deploying optical fiber internet nationwide won't be quick or easy.

You're right, Shivanya. It's a tough task to establish a nationwide internet service in under a year. Okay, I'll get started.

The Next Day

EMILINK hits its lower circuit within the first hour of trading.

Shivanya, lower circuit.

I know, Susan; it's an inevitable outcome after yesterday's disaster. Tell Upadhyay Ji to have his report ready. I'm on my way to the office.

So, Upadhyay Ji, what's your take on EMILINK shares collapsing?

Ma'am, after thoroughly analyzing the data regarding EMILINK's sell-off, I've made some key observations:

1. Selling occurred randomly; no indicators or movements in technical charts suggested retail traders should short the stock, yet it still fell. This indicates intentional manipulation.

2. I initially suspected illegal activity, but all seller accounts are legitimate. However, they all belong to one investment firm: SOLTRADE, and AVCL is currently managing their market operations, suggesting HFT involvement by AVCL.

Aarav! How could I be so naïve? Of course, Aarav orchestrated this.

I never thought he'd stoop this low just for revenge. It's so petty and mean-spirited. I was right about him—he's just a downgraded person who managed to earn money but clearly lacks class.

Great work, Upadhyay Ji. Can you do me a favor? Tell Lakshya to talk to our investors and ensure we buy EMILINK shares in bulk. I want to stop this sell-off and assure them we'll repay them in the future.

I won't let that cheap creep mess with my father's firm.

Understood, ma'am. I'm on it. Just one question: If this is about revenge, why create a fake sell-off when you know the Sen Group owns EMILINK? They'll recover soon, making the whole point of revenge pointless.

Upadhyay Ji, sometimes revenge isn't about causing real harm; it's just to show someone that you can strike back whenever you want. It's an upset mindset, nothing more.

But he doesn't realize we have people like you to protect us. Now we know where to focus—just keep an eye on what AVCL is doing and report everything back to me.

Aarav! What's the update, Sharma Ji?

The fruit is ripe for picking.

Great, Sharma Ji. What about regulatory clearance?

Aarav, the minister wants to meet you first before deciding on approval.

Fantastic! Just secure an appointment with Minister Ji. I'll meet him tomorrow or whenever we can.

I'm honored to meet you, Minister.

Yes, Mr. Aarav. I wanted to discuss your SATNET project. What are your actual intentions with this initiative? This technology is new to our country, and I need to be confident that it complies with all regulations.

Sir, the idea behind SATNET is simple. This technology is widely used abroad; why should our country be left behind? We're fully capable of becoming a leader in the space sector.

I want my country to be the first to benefit from this technology before sharing it with the world. We will no longer be followers; it's time for us to lead the next generation of technological innovation.

SATNET is a powerful step in that direction. It will provide internet access to remote areas where traditional services struggle to reach due to geographical challenges.

You're right, Aarav; India will lead now. It's time for us to reclaim our rightful place, whether in space or any other sector. I entered politics to see our country dominate the world.

My father dreamed of seeing India excel in technology and becoming a pioneer in future advancements.

SATNET has the full support of the government. We will utilize it to provide internet services to every corner of the country. It will be part of the Connect India scheme.

You're an inspiration, Sir. At such a young age, you're striving to transform our nation. We've always been guided by the wisdom of our ancestors to build a better tomorrow.

I'm honored to invite you to be our Chief Guest at the launch of SATNET and SATSPACE satellite on October 30th.

Great, Aarav! That's right before Diwali—what an awesome day for a launch! SATNET will have the guidance of the National Space Agency for its launch, and we'll roll out SATNET then.

Indeed, Sir.

October 20th

Shivanya!

What is it, Susan?

Your dad had a heart attack.

What are you saying, Susan? How did this happen? Where is he?

We're taking him to the hospital. I'm coming, Susan; please take care of him until I arrive.

Shivanya rushed to the hospital, anxious.

What happened to my father? Where is he?

Don't worry, Shivanya. Your father is under observation; he had a heart attack.

How could this happen? He's so fit!

Shivanya, lately his eating habits have been a bit erratic, and the stress from the EMILINK share situation has had a cumulative effect.

But my father never lets stress affect his health!

Sometimes, even the most disciplined person can slip. If you ask me why, it's because he's human.

Don't worry; your father will be fine. Stay calm; that's the most important thing.

Doctor, how's my father? Shivanya asked the doctor who emerged from the ICU.

Ms. Sen, he's fine; it was just a mild heart attack. However, he needs to be monitored for 1-2 days. No visitors for now—no pressure on his mind. Mild heart attacks can be deceptive; they seem harmless but may indicate serious issues ahead.

Okay, Doctor. I'll follow your advice.

It's been two days, and I haven't seen my father. This feels awful.

Shivanya, calm down. We're following the doctor's orders.

Shivanya Sen!

Yes, Doctor?

Please come to my office.

What is it, Doctor?

We've done all the tests and diagnoses. He's stable and out of danger, but I suspect he may experience a fatal heart attack in the near future.

Why, Doctor?

Because this was a Sudden Cardiac Arrest, and SCAs are hard to predict. An unexpected rise in blood pressure due to sudden shock or trauma can lead to this.

In his case, sudden shock is likely the cause of the SCA.

Doctor, what's the solution?

Shivanya, we'll keep him under constant monitoring through a three-phase plan. First, he'll need another week in the hospital for advanced care. Next, we'll implement three months of nursing care at home. Once we're sure the SCA was an isolated incident and his heart, blood pressure, and other metrics are stable, we'll move to the third step: monthly heart checks for nine months.

Only after nearly a year of monitoring can we confidently say he's fine and can continue living his life. A stent has already been placed in his heart to prevent blockage—standard procedure.

However, all other passages are also at risk of blockages. I want to avoid surgeries or bypasses, which is why we have this three-phase care program.

Shivanya, be extremely cautious—no stressful activities that could spike his blood pressure. Surviving an SCA is tough, and thankfully, he did.

Doctor, I will ensure that every instruction you give is followed strictly. I'll do whatever it takes to get my dad back to health in less than a year.

October 30th - SATNET Launch

Today marks a historic moment as SATSKY prepares to become the first private space company to launch a satellite using its own rocket. The National Space Agency has provided essential guidance for this launch, and there's buzz that the Minister and SATSKY promoter, Aarav, will announce something significant. Everyone is eager to find out what's in store—Aarav seems to have something big planned for SATSKY's launch. Stay tuned to VMEDIA for updates!

Mayur?

Aarav, we're all set! The launch will start in 30 minutes.

Great, Mayur! You're in control now. Make our country proud; you're at the heart of a new chapter in history. Let's show everyone what our youth can achieve!

Aarav, how are you?

I'm good, Minister Ji. So?

Sir, the launch is set for T-30 minutes. SATSKY has an impressive setup; everything about this launch looks promising.

Indeed, Sir. This proves that if we invest in our country's talent, we will never be disappointed.

Look over there—that's Mayur, CEO of SATSKY. He's a brilliant guy. I'm impressed, Aarav. The government should support initiatives that develop technology like this on a larger scale.

T-10 Minutes to Launch

What's the weather status?

Mayur, the weather is favorable for launch.

Great! Any glitches in any systems, Noval?

Negative, Mayur. Everything looks good.

Launch mode initiated.

Final countdown begins: 10, 9, 8, 7, 6, 5, 4, 3, 2, 1.

The SATSKY rocket launched flawlessly from the pad, and the crowd erupted in cheers—an emotional and historic moment!

Aarav, it's done! Congratulations, Mayur and the SATSKY team—well done! We've launched the first satellite via a private rocket; it's a dream come true, Aarav!

I know Mayur.

Minister Ji at the Press Conference after the Successful Launch:

Today, we witnessed history. SATSKY became the first private company to launch a satellite into space. This is a monumental achievement, not just for SATSKY but for India as a whole. We've often been seen as a country that follows rather than leads.

This SATSKY launch is not just about sending a satellite; it's about launching India's journey to greatness.

I'm privileged to announce SATNET today. The SATSKY launch will create a constellation for satellite-based internet services in our country. SATNET will cater to various industries, providing them with access to advanced internet technology. The key point about SATNET is that it's a flagship program under the Government of India's Connect India scheme, aimed at providing free internet access to remote regions.

SATNET represents a revolutionary advancement, significantly reducing the time it takes for traditional internet services to reach rural areas, while allowing the government to expand this coverage nationwide.

All remote regions or areas with internet access delays can now benefit from SATNET.

I also want to express my gratitude to Aarav, the promoter of SATSKY. He played a crucial role in making this happen on such short notice. Thank you, Aarav, for partnering with the government in this initiative.

Shivanya?

What is it, Dad?

Can you please turn on the television? I want updates on the country and the market.

Dad, you just got out of the hospital, and you want to access the very source of your stress? Why would you share my health plan with the doctor?

He doesn't know, but I do—you're the strictest person I know!

Shivanya, I'll get bored! You've handed all my business affairs over to the COO for a year. What do you expect me to do—sit around?

I don't know, Dad. Go for a walk or engage in activities you've avoided due to time constraints. It's better to take this break and enjoy life a little.

Actually, Shivanya, it's good this happened now. I can fully enjoy your engagement and wedding!

Listen, Dad, I've postponed the engagement and wedding for a year.

Why, Shivanya? When did this happen?

Dad, I need a complete year of rest—no fancy activities. I can get married next year; there's no hurry. You worry too much about me.

Okay, if you've decided to postpone, then I'll respect your wishes.

But please, just turn on the television.

You know I can't refuse when you ask like that.

Okay, but I'll join you.

Sure, why not!

Breaking News on VMedia! Today's historic launch of the SATSKY satellite is just the tip of the iceberg. Minister Ji has also unveiled SATNET, a satellite-based internet service that will revolutionize connectivity across the country. The satellite launched by SATSKY is a flagship initiative under the India Connect scheme, promising internet access to every sector. Aarav, the mastermind behind this project, has shaken up the internet service industry. Who would have imagined that within a year, we'd have a live satellite-based internet service in India?

This confirms that Aarav isn't just an ordinary businessman; he's in a league of his own. With SATNET, he's not only transformed the internet service landscape but has also partnered with the government to provide free internet access to remote areas—a move that positions SATNET as a major player in the market and builds its reputation for reliability.

However, EMILINK shares have taken a nosedive following this announcement, signaling a setback in their internet service expansion plans. They're going to have a tough time competing now.

My God! Is this what he was plotting? He played us! Disgusting, Aarav!

What happened, Shivanya?

Father, you know our share debacle was orchestrated by AVCL, which Aarav owns. I thought he did it out of revenge for my previous insult.

But he actually wanted me to suspect him so I'd pressure Lakshya to shift focus to telecom and halt our expansion plans. He knew how I would react and made sure I had all the evidence I needed.

Shivanya, I have to admit, I'm impressed.

Why, Father? Impressed by what?

After all these years, I'm seeing a businessman operate in a way that's truly innovative. He's a genius. He played the market like a decoy while keeping his real plans under wraps—that's what you call strategy!

He anticipated your reaction to the share drop and proved you right. While you all were distracted by this temporary market situation, he was busy acquiring a firm, bringing the government on board, and securing regulatory approval. We need to ensure that launch happens as soon as possible!

Shivanya, if you're surrounded by brilliant businessmen, you'll evolve and grow as a businessman yourself. Aarav's decision-making at such a young age is powerful. He knows where to invest his money.

So now you're praising him? What's next? You want to make him your son-in-law?

No, I'm not suggesting that, but as a businessman, I'm genuinely impressed. Speaking of my son-in-law, where's Lakshya?

He's tied up with the EMILINK business. Tell him he's in hot water. Forget the meeting and come up with a creative plan to compete with SATNET.

After this news, he'll feel the same pressure I'm feeling. I told both of you that business isn't just about logistics and deep pockets. All your investors knew Shaurya Sen was backing EMILINK, which is why they invested heavily. Then Lakshya focused on logistics to distribute SIM cards nationwide.

In telecom, that strategy might work, but it won't in every business. You both lacked creativity; no one in EMILINK thought beyond the traditional approach. Your product must resonate and connect with the modern world. I'm telling you, Shivanya, SATNET is going to be a game-changer. We need to rethink EMILINK's future.

As far as I know, Dad, you liked Lakshya?

Did I ever mention that, Shivanya? What do you mean? You don't think I like him?

Shivanya, Lakshya is a good guy, but I was never entirely sure about him as my son-in-law. I thought you liked him, and you saw him as someone from our class and status.

Shivanya, my father worked as a migrant laborer before starting a construction firm, so I can't talk about class or luxury. True class is about how you face challenges in life.

Father, you never told me about this!

After your mother left, I immersed myself in work and didn't spend enough time with you. That's why you don't know this side of my life.

Shivanya, money is important when used for good—investing in technology and building for the future. If you have people around you who genuinely care without ulterior motives, that's something no amount of money can buy.

Today, most people around us have obligations but don't really care about us like your mother did. It's a blessing to have such people in your life who offer more value than money.

I'm surprised to hear all of this, Dad. Now enough talking; you've taken your pills. Get some rest!

Shivanya is now deep in thought about Aarav and how his eyes lit up whenever she was around.

Eight Months Later…….

SATNET has taken the market by storm, with Aarav becoming the youngest and richest man in the country. His partnerships in cloud computing, HFT, and other tech ventures utilizing SATNET's satellite system have skyrocketed his business to staggering heights.

Knock, knock.

Can I come in, Uncle?

Neil, my son, come in! How are you, Sen Uncle?

I'm doing well, fully recovered and ready to dive back into business.

That's great news! Neil, I can't express how happy I am to see you after all these years. How's my friend, Senior Ahuja?

He's doing fine.

I never thought you'd come to see me, Neil.

Uncle, ever since I heard about your recovery, I thought a lot about us. In the end, my affection won out. You and Shivanya have always felt like family to me.

Misunderstandings happen in close families; it's important for someone to take the first step to mend things. As the younger one, I felt it was my duty to reach out.

You're making me emotional, Neil. You did the right thing. I know I should have supported your father when he needed it, but I got so caught up in business that I lost sight of the human side.

Both Neil and Sen Uncle share a heartfelt hug, tears in their eyes.

I want in on this warm hug!

Shivanya said, entering the room.

Come on, Shivanya!

Neil said, creating a lovely family moment.

I'm really sorry, Shivanya, for being so rude to you.

Neil, you're like an older brother to me; you have every right to feel that way.

No, Shivanya, you've always treated my father and me like family. I shouldn't have acted that way, so I sincerely apologize.

Enough with the apologies, Neil! I'm just so happy to see you and Uncle together again. I'll bring Shabby next time; she's excited to meet you.

That's the first thing I want to do—see my future daughter-in-law and bless you both for your wedding!

I'll also visit your father and my best friend, Senior Ahuja, separately. I can't wait to see his reaction after so many years.

I'm thrilled that our family is finally coming together.

I told you, Shivanya, sometimes troubles bring lessons that change our lives for the better. Now, you take a rest, Uncle; I'll take my leave.

Okay, Neil, take care, my son.

Wait, Neil; I need to talk to you!

Shivanya said.

Yes, what is it?

How's everything?

You mean, how's Aarav?

Don't look surprised; I know everything since you two met at my wedding.

Aarav is doing well! He's achieved something most can only dream of. I never thought a guy who was a waiter just a few years ago would become the richest man in the country. It's legendary! Aarav's life is a classic example of what one can achieve when you leave doubts behind and believe in yourself.

Shivanya, he's an amazing guy. Even after liking you so much, he let you go because you wanted that. I can see the curiosity in you—you like him too! So stop wasting time and go for it.

Neil, why are you pushing me?

You're my sister; I want you to be happy, and I know you'd be happy with Aarav. I'll do whatever it takes to help you realize that.

By the way, there's a farewell party organized by Aarav today for Nitya.

Nitya? Who's that?

She's a special girl going abroad for her undergrad program on a scholarship.

That's great! But how are Nitya and Aarav connected?

Aarav and Nitya grew up in the same orphanage. Aarav worked hard to pay for her schooling because he treated her like a younger sister. Now she's off to advance her education in technology abroad. We're all so proud of her, especially Aarav, so today's her farewell party.

I'll take my leave now. Take care, Shivanya!

Love is brewing, and it's at the point where the pressure cooker is about to whistle!

The Nitya Farewell Party..........

"Congratulations, my little sister!"

"Thanks, brother! What an incredible farewell party you've organized for me."

"You totally deserve this. And hey, congrats to you too!"

"Why, for Nitya?"

"Because you're officially the richest man in the country! I can't believe I'm witnessing this."

Aarav smiled. "This party is all about you, Nitya. Being the richest is just a temporary title."

"Hi, Mr. Billionaire! How do I avoid being mocked by my ex-boss?"

"Ex-boss? Once a boss, always a boss!"

"So proud of you for how far you've come."

"Aarav!!!"

"Shabby."

"Richest man in the room! You deserve this! You're a kickass businessman! I told Neil when you launched AVCL that you'd make it big."

"Thanks a lot, Shabby. I owe a lot of this to all of you."

"Where's Nitya?"

"She's right there. You two go meet her. I'll check the arrangements."

"Nitya, my little princess, you've made us all proud!"

"Thanks, Neil and Shabby. You two look stunning!"

"You mean I look fab and Neil is just okay?"

"No, Neil, you look great too!"

"Is that so? If you say so. My only advice, Nitya: have fun and everything else will follow."

"Thanks, Neil. My brother is a legend—waiter to the richest!"

"Aarav, I can't decide if I should drink all night or dive into a pool of wine!"

"I'm so happy!"

"Thanks, Sri, but hold your horses. We need to finish this party; it's Nitya's farewell!"

"Yes, Aarav. She's grown up so fast. I still remember when we used to drop her off at school. And now she's going abroad!"

"Where's the famous Sharma Ji, Aarav?"

"Neil asked."

"Sharma Ji went on a world tour with Mrs. Sharma."

"Wow, a world tour? Even at his age, he's so romantic, fulfilling his wife's wishes!"

"Indeed, Shabby. Speaking of romance, how's yours going?"

"What romance, Shabby?"

"Listen, Mr. I won't reveal my love life. Sri spilled the beans the day you met Shivanya at your wedding!"

"I'm telling you, Shabby, it's nothing. How could it be? Shivanya is classy, with standards and manners. I'm just...different."

"Why did you let her go when you knew she liked you?"

"Shabby, I can't just hold her hand because I like her. I want Shivanya to feel the same way. In her world, I'm just a waiter. Marrying a waiter is never part of her dream."

"Don't give me that nonsense, Aarav! You were already building AVCL and had achieved enough status that she must be okay with it."

"That's not the case, Shabby. We have a history. No matter who I become, she'll always see me as the waiter."

"This is crazy, Aarav. I never thought you'd give up on her so easily. Everyone knows you started all this after meeting her. If she doesn't see it, you should make an effort to help her realize."

"Shabby, I've felt a connection between us, but if she truly understood how I felt..."

"How do you know I didn't understand how you felt about me?"

Shivanya said as she entered the farewell party.

"Shivanya, how come you're here?"

"That's not answering my question, Aarav. It's because I know you don't like me."

Shivanya looked into Aarav's eyes. "How can a guy who stared at me fearlessly when we first met be so insecure about the fact that I don't like him?"

"You know, Aarav, I've always dreamed of finding a man with whom I can share a genuine connection—a comfort zone where I can be my true self, unfiltered. Whenever we met, I felt that connection and comfort with you. I don't know why, but I've always been curious about what you're up to. I've never felt this way about anyone before."

"Shivanya, why are you saying all this now?"

"Because it's my turn to give you the same lecture you gave me about being unaware of my feelings, blah blah. And one more thing: I don't let go of what I truly want."

"What are you saying, Shivanya? You're getting engaged to Lakshya!"

"That engagement is postponed and will never happen."

"What happened?"

"No more words, Aarav. I'll talk; you'll listen. Learn some manners for heaven's sake."

"Sorry, Shivanya, I'm all ears."

Shivanya went down on one knee and said, "Mr. Aarav, I love you with all my heart and soul. Will you marry me?"

Aarav was speechless for a moment, and everyone eagerly waited for his response.

"Aarav, say it! I love you too; my knees are hurting!"

"Shivanya, I love you too."

The crowd erupted in applause. Shivanya and Aarav hugged, filled with love and passion.

"I never imagined you'd come back into my life, Shivanya."

"Who said I was gone?"

"Don't you have eyes? You pathetic waiter! How dare you spill tea on my dress? Do you have any idea how much this costs? More than your annual salary, you idiot!"

Shivanya and Aarav shared a laugh at the scene.

"What a story, Dad."

"Indeed, it is, Shovik. But it's more than just a story; it's a lesson. Life throws hurdles your way, but with the right mindset and approach, you can overcome any challenge. Never be afraid to try and fail; success is just a byproduct. What matters is your response. If you understand the process of reaction, the product will follow naturally."

"Now I have to go pick up your mother; she's coming home from abroad."

"But, Dad, I want to know what happened with Lakshya and where Aarav and Shivanya are now!"

"Enough for today, son. For the rest of the story, ask your mother. If I'm Neil Ahuja witnessing this, your mother is Shabby Ahuja, who knows everything. So, take her help. Bye, Shovik. And always remember..."

"Keep pulling the strings, no matter how high they are..."